Tom Costigan is a washed-out mercenary, stuck cleaning dishes for a hole-in-the-wall bar despite his chrome arm and the computer in his head. While having a smoke break in the alley out back, he's approached by a former comrade. His former commander is putting the old team back together for a big corporate heist.

Tom isn't big on asking questions, and the money's attractive enough to make him jump for it. But when the hand-off to the buyers goes south and the bullets start to fly, Tom finds himself with a sealed container and the payout.

But the payout is encrypted, and he doesn't know what's in the container.

Even with the help of his hacker sister, will Tom be able to stay ahead of his former comrades, the buyers, and the people they stole from and why is everyone willing to kill for what looks like a bunch of silver goop?

This edition first published 2022 by Fahrenheit Press.

ISBN: 978-1-914475-30-6

10 9 8 7 6 5 4 3 2 1

www.Fahrenheit-Press.com

F 4 E

Project Prometheus

By

Matthew X. Gomez

Fahrenheit Press

To Kelly, for everything.

ONE

Tom stepped out into the alley behind Danzig's, a cold misty rain dripping down from on high, city lights gleaming off the titanium and chrome of his left arm. He ducked under an overhang, filched a half-crumpled pack of cigarettes out of his pocket.

He held up his fake thumb, a blue propane flame cutting up into the night and then extinguished. He took a long, satisfied drag. Someone cleared their throat.

Tom leaned back and closed his eyes, took another long drag, filling his lungs with smoke.

"You're a hard man to track down." A figure stepped out from the shadows, long black trench coat hanging down over a spare frame. Blue-black hair tied back from a square face. The light caught the silver implants around his eyes. "A man didn't know better, I'd say you didn't want to be found."

Tom grunted. "Shaman. This a social call?"

Shaman shook his head. "Wouldn't be bothering you just to say 'hi.' Thought you might be interested in getting some paying work."

Tom's eyes narrowed and he held up his left arm. "This coming from you or from O'Dell? Last time I worked for O'Dell I picked up this little souvenir."

Shaman nodded. "It's from Sam all right. He got the old crew back together. Promises a nice pay day. Better than washing dishes anyway."

Tom snorted. "'Course it does." He took another drag on his cigarette, jabbed his thumb back to the door. "I don't get shot washing dishes though."

Shaman smiled, lips pulling back from even teeth. "I suppose there's that, isn't there?" He pulled a card from a pocket, flipped it through the air to Tom, the light reflecting off the shiny black surface. Tom snatched it out of the air with his flesh and blood hand. Embossed in chrome on the card was a telephone number.

"What's this?"

"An invitation," Shaman replied. "If you change your mind, give it a call."

"Yeah." Tom slipped the card into his jeans. "What's the deadline?"

"Sam needs an answer by the weekend. This is a limited time engagement, and he needs to know if he has to look at other talent."

"Yeah? He's got someone else lined up?"

"Maybe." Shaman's grin disappeared. "You're his first choice though. Took a couple of weeks to track you down here. You're good at hiding your tracks."

"Not good enough, obviously," Tom mumbled around his cigarette.

Shaman laughed. "I can't even take credit for finding you. Ju-Won did that."

Tom wrinkled his nose. "He's in on this too?"

Shaman nodded. "The entire crew is on this. Anatoliy and Rayen as well."

Tom hawked spit and left a wet smear on the asphalt. He watched it swirl with the rain, become indistinguishable from the rest of the water headed toward the storm drain. "This backed by Defiant Strategy?"

Shaman shook his head. "They went bust after the Venezuela shitstorm. Strictly an independent operation this time."

Tom's eyes went flat and he fingered the card in his pocket. "What's he looking to steal?"

Shaman smiled, but didn't touch his eyes. He stepped backward into the shadow until he was nothing but a shadow among the shadows. "Call the number if you're interested, Tom. You're wasted here among the civvies."

"I get shot a lot less on this job," Tom called out, but Shaman's only answer was to laugh.

Tom pulled the card out, twisted it in his calloused fingers. "Shit." He shoved the card back into his pocket and walked back inside to finish the rest of his shift, a tingling sense of dread creeping up his spine, long buried nightmares of the LatAm Wars struggling to the surface.

TWO

"What are you going to do when you get out?" Ju-Won asked, his head obscured by the VR headset he wore. He'd spliced into the local network, but given the deplorable state of the local infrastructure, he'd spent more time smoking cigarettes and cursing then he did actually monitoring the local situation.

"Get out of where? Here? Caracas?" Tom asked. He frowned down at his empty pack of cigarettes, tried to remember when he smoked the last one. "My contract doesn't expire for what, another three years? Probably re-up if I've got the option."

"He means out of this mess." Anatoliy's voice rumbled like an avalanche. It had taken Tom a couple of weeks to get used to the big man's thick Ukrainian accent. "If any of us had any useful skill, we wouldn't be working for Defiant Strategy, would we?"

They were sitting in the stripped ballroom of a hotel, the plaster peeling from walls pockmarked with bullet holes. Artillery rumbled in the distance, setting the already precarious chandelier trembling. Tom knew it wasn't going to be an easy assignment as soon as Sam told him what it was going to entail. Tom glanced sideways toward him. Sam O'Dell, veteran mercenary. Started out as one of Uncle Sam's Misguided Children, but got drummed out on a dishonorable. Trouble with Sam was he liked combat too much. As long as bullets were firing, Sam was your guy. Trouble came when peace broke out, and Sam wasn't sure what to do with himself.

Right now though he had his large brimmed safari hat tucked down over his eyes, his assault rifle propped up next to him. From the way Sam's lips twitched up in a smile under his mustache, Tom knew he wasn't asleep.

Tom came from a different background, young tough from the city, running with one gang or another. He'd thought about going with the military, but somehow the thought of taking orders didn't sit right with him. Never mind he'd set out to prove himself a good loyal soldier on the streets of his neighborhood.

He got picked up for the illegal possession of a handgun, a piece the local mechanic had set to autofire. That meant a stint in a corporate sponsored rehabilitation facility. Ostensibly, the prisoners were housed by the corporation, performed whatever manual labor they needed done at a fraction of the cost. Sure, they were supposed to get paid, but most of what they made went toward housing and feeding them, with the little that was left going to the commissary.

The prison made for prime recruiting ground. The white collar hacks were picked up, given a better education in terms of where they went wrong. Those in for the more violent offenses were given a different choice, provided they could toe the line. Those that couldn't served as an object lesson.

Sam was Tom's recruiting officer, looking sharp in his suit, an expensive cigar clenched between his teeth. Tom remembered seeing Sam standing there with one of the COs, up on a catwalk staring down at the convicts, stabbing with his finger at likely prospects. Tom made sure he got noticed, as signing the corporate contract meant a commutation of sentence.

Tom sniffed. "I've got plenty of useful skills," he said.

Ju-Won laughed, his head swiveling blindly in his VR headset. "Yeah, what can you do other than breaking things?"

"Hey now," Anatoliy retorted. "That's all some of us good at. And be glad we are, because where would you be otherwise? Driving a desk probably."

"Better than sitting in this dump with you dogs," Ju-Won replied.

"Any chatter out there?" Sam asked, not lifting his hat from his head.

Ju-Won spat. "Hard to tell. Shaman, you see anything?"

"That's a negative," Shaman's voice crackled in Tom's earpiece. He'd stationed himself with his sniper rifle up at the top of the hotel in order to check sight lines. "I think we're clear at the moment. Just me and the mosquitos. How's our guest?"

Tom glanced at the person they were supposed to be protecting. He sat with his back against the wall, his eyes wide and bloodshot, his suit torn and dirty. His eyes darted nervous and quick from one mercenary to the next, never mind their contract was to protect him. Tom didn't have all the details, but he was reasonably certain the man was part of the government that had just collapsed. The man was a client of Defiant Strategy, but they were there purely in a bodyguard capacity.

4

No one had said anything about a counter-revolution.

"Looks like he's about to shit himself," Tom replied.

"Don't be too hard on him," Anatoliy said. Another rumble of artillery shook the building. "Not everyone is suited to this kind of life."

Tom shook his head. He closed his eyes and lay back against his pack. "So long as we get paid, right? Any idea if Rayen's found us a way out yet?"

"Ju-Won?" Sam asked.

"That's a negative. Good ole U. S. of A. has the entire airspace designated no fly. We're stuck unless you've got another way out of here."

The sound of a rifle being fired echoed through their earpieces.

"Shaman, what the hell was that?"

"Company," came the reply, the sniper's voice calm and even. "About two dozen people converging on the hotel, and they are looking mighty unfriendly." Another shot rang out. "They've got cover now and closing in."

"Roger that, see if you can keep them busy," Sam replied. He was on his feet, eyes alert, as if he'd been fully awake the entire time. "Anatoliy?"

"Yes, yes." The big man pulled back a tarp, revealing a heavy-caliber machine gun with an attached tripod. He hefted it up in his arms. "Which way are they coming from Shaman?"

"Check the West. You're going to want to set up over there."

"Alright."

"Tom? Head over there as well. Anatoliy, find a spot on the second floor. Tom, I want you on the first floor," Sam said. "Ju-won, get that fucking thing off and watch our guest. Last thing we need is for him to get spooked and run off on us. Because the way this whole thing has gone that is exactly what I'd expect to have happen."

Ju-Won put down the headset and packed it away, then pulled out a stubby bull-pup shotgun. "Hear that? We get to be buddies," he said with a grin that revealed too many cracked and uneven teeth. The client looked somewhat less than assured. The client scooted back further to the wall, hugged his knees to his chest.

Tom checked his submachinegun as he took position. As long as it wasn't a major push, he felt he had enough ammunition, and he figured the hotel was a low profile enough target that the artillery would leave it alone. He almost felt bad for the ones who were supposed to be supporting the government. He knew though that were as many mercenaries aiding the revolutionaries as were supporting the failing government. He set up behind the battered front desk, lining up magazines of ammunition and three grenades in preparation. It would have been better if Defiant had provided proper combat webbing, but Tom had come to realize that whoever ran logistics had never been in a fire fight. They'd previously mined the back entrances in case anyone tried to come through there. The city still had power, and there were enough lights on to cast enough shadows to be distracting. Still, it was better than the pitch black of the jungle. Tom would take city fighting over that nightmare any day.

"You set, Tom?" Shaman's voice came through loud and clear, crackling in his earpiece.

"Yeah. No movement yet." Tom kept his voice pitched low. If someone was out there, he didn't want anyone to hear it.

"Keep your eyes open and your mouths shut, boys," Sam said.

Tom spotted a shadow creeping from a fountain toward the front door. "I've got movement," he hissed.

"Let them get to the door," Sam replied. "Then light them up."

Tom braced the stock of his gun against his shoulder, kept his breathing slow and steady. The windows of the hotel had long been shattered, the broken glass still scattered on the ground. He saw a figure step through the entrance, heard the crunch of glass under a boot. Tom pulled the trigger, the gun barking in his hand. He kept control, a short controlled burst. Gunfire answered back, and he kept low, bullets smacking into the furniture and chewing through the desk.

Tom heard Anatoliy open up with the machinegun, the harsh chatter nearly drowning out the screams. Tom grabbed the magazines and grenades and crawled to a different position. He poked his head around the corner, let out another burst that caught a woman trying to come through a broken window.

"We've got a problem, boss," Shaman said, his voice possessing an edge Tom wasn't comfortable hearing. Tom heard an explosion come from the back of the building. "They're bringing up some technicals."

Tom could see the pickup trucks entering the front plaza, headlights blazing through the darkness. Mounted on the back of each was a machinegun, and he was pretty sure he spotted the silhouette of a rocket launcher.

"Understood. Tom, Anatoliy, pull back."

"Boss?"

"Now Anatoliy." Tom scooped up the ammunition and grenades, hustled back to the ballroom. He kept his head low. The sound that followed was deafening as the machineguns opened up, ripping through the walls and the desk as if they were paper. The ballroom wasn't much better, and the whole building shook as a rocket detonated somewhere inside, dust filling the interior with a choking cloud of debris.

"Everyone okay?" Sam's voice came over the ear piece.

"All in one piece," Shaman responded.

"Slightly dinged," Anatoliy replied.

"Tom?"

"Yeah, I'm here, just some ringing in my ears."

"Good, can you get to the roof?"

Tom heard someone coming up behind him. He turned letting out a short burst from his gun and sprinted for the stairs. The return fire punched through brick and plaster. Tom felt a sting on the back of his leg followed by a warm wet trickle, realized he'd been grazed by a bullet or a piece of shrapnel.

He pulled the pin on one of his grenades and tossed it through the doorway he'd gone through. He took the stairs two at a time, putting distance between himself and the attackers. "Uh, boss, are you sure that's such a good idea?"

"Don't question me, boy," Sam barked back.

Tom shut his mouth and hustled up the stairs. Beneath him, he could hear the attackers enter the stairwell. He pulled another grenade, gave it a two count and gave it a soft underarm pitch. The dull whump of the explosion preceded a cloud of smoke billowing out into the hallway. Tom pulled his goggles down over his eyes and a bandana up over his mouth, his leg hurting each time he put pressure down on it. He burst onto the roof, slammed the door behind him. Anatoliy came over, slid a bit of metal in place to bar the door closed. Sam, Shaman, Ju-Won and the client sat on top of the roof. Down below more gunmen rushed into the building.

"That's not going to stop them," Tom gasped, pointing at the flimsy barricade. "Where are we supposed to go from here?"

Sam smiled. "Rayen came through."

"Thought you said it was a no fly zone?"

Sam's smile broadend. "Funny thing happens when you tell a woman like Rayen 'no.' Suddenly she finds all kinds of ways to make it possible. We just need to hold out for about five minutes."

Tom felt his stomach drop. "I'm not sure we have five minutes, sir."

"Clear a way," Anatoliy said, deploying his machinegun across the roof to face the barred door.

Tom dropped back behind Anatoliy. He ejected the magazine from his gun, checked the bullet count and slammed it back home. He was down to one grenade, and he wasn't sure it was going to make a difference. Shaman set up on the other side of the big Ukranian, trading his sniper rifle for a pistol. Ju-Won held back with the client, his shotgun cradled in his arms.

"Tom, when that door opens, I need you to place that grenade right in that hole, you understand? Don't miss."

Tom looked up from where he was bandaging his leg. "Yeah, I got it."

"Anatoliy, as soon as that grenade goes off, you open up."

"Understood."

"Ju-Won, you got ears on Rayen yet?"

"Not yet, boss. I'll let you know as soon as I do, but there's a lot of chatter out there right now."

Sam nodded. "See if you can cut through any of it. She said she was coming in hot."

"I know, I know," Ju-Won replied, running a hand over his head and tugging sharply on his ponytail. "I'm the one that told you."

"Yeah, yeah. How's the client?"

Ju-Won shrugged. "Still alive. Pretty catatonic otherwise."

"Yeah, well make sure he stays out of the way, all right?"

"That won't be a problem."

An explosion rocked the hotel, sending the entire building swaying. The door exploded outward, metal pinwheeling into the air in razor shards. Tom pitched the grenade straight at the opening, landing it in the middle of the gunmen surging out on to the roof. Anatoliy, prone on the roof, pulled the trigger on the machinegun. The gunmen, some of them, fell back, bodies torn and bloody. Something surged forward then, propelling the bodies forward like dolls before a bulldozer. A figure pushed through the dead and dying, all metal and chrome.

"Shit, they got a cyborg," Sam yelled. Anatoliy trained his fire on it, as did Tom. He wished he had held on to another grenade. The machinegun rounds pinged and dented the metal composite body, and then Anatoliy was running for cover as the man-machine hybrid dropped to one knee, a rocket launcher sliding into position from its back to its shoulder.

Tom felt the bile burn in his throat. Cyborgs were supposed to be strictly verboten in combat, but the Geneva Convention had long been a stranger in Caracas. Tom had to wonder how much of the man was still alive and aware in the metallic shell. Not that it made much difference when one of them was trying to kill you.

A fiery plume shot forward, exploding on the roof and wrecking the machinegun. Tom slid to one side, hoping to flank the cyborg. He dove for cover as the cyborg brought his assault rifle around, tracer rounds arcing toward him, slicing through the industrial fans on the roof. A sharp pain shot through his left arm, and he bit back a curse. He tried to get his arm back on his weapon, but for some reason it didn't seem to want to work, so he fired it off one handed. Bullets bounced off like raindrops. The cyborg got back to its feet. Something sailed through the air, stuck to its metal casing. It had long enough to look down before the charge detonated, cratering its armor and sending it to the ground, a look of profound disbelief on its face.

"Here comes Rayen!" Ju-Won shouted.

A VTOL craft skimmed over the ground, hugging the horizon line as it deftly dipped and swayed among the buildings. Occasional bursts of fire lanced up from the ground, but the craft was moving too quickly for any to connect. The craft braked over the rooftop, Tom and the others giving it a wide enough berth as it hovered just over the top of the hotel.

"Go, go, go!" Sam yelled, helping to hoist his crew up into the passenger compartment. Rayen sat in the pilot seat, her helmet pressed down tight over her mohawk, a fierce grin on her face as she trained the autocannons mounted on the wings on the gunmen.

"Oh fuck!" Tom moaned as Sam tried to grab him by the wreck of his left arm.

"Jesus, Anatoliy, give me a hand with Tom here. Come on, get him in before he bleeds out."

"Huh?" Tom asked, looking at his arm for the first time. From the shoulder down it was a mess of shredded meat and shattered bones. Anatoliy leaned down, grabbed Tom under the shoulders, and hoisted him into the craft. Tom tried to keep from screaming, and failed.

"Everyone in?" Rayen called back.

"Yeah, that's everyone, including the client," Sam confirmed.

Ju-Won opened his laptop on his computer, typed a short line of code as Sam used a pair of scissors to cut away at Tom's shirt as Anatoliy held him down. Shaman stared out into the distance. Tom wanted to say something, but then Sam jabbed him with a needle and he felt like a heavy warm blanket swaddled him, and he felt as if he floated above the pain, detached and separate.

"Boss. Just got word that the client's contract has been terminated," Ju-Won said.

"Is that right? Shaman."

"No, no, there is some misunderstanding," the man said, a dark stain appearing on the front of his pants.

Shaman smiled at the man, then grabbed him and threw him out of the craft. It was moving fast enough that his scream was cut short and Tom didn't hear him hit the ground. He closed his eyes and let the synthetic opiate wrap itself like a warm blanket around him.

THREE

The phone rang in Tom's skull, Sunny's number floating in his vision, superimposed over the crack in his ceiling.

"Tom? Christ, do you know what time it is?" Sunny didn't have her camera turned on, so all he saw was her smiling face haloed by orange hair. He thought she'd had dyed it purple the last time he'd seen her.

"Uhm, late? How are you Sunny?"

"Well I was sleeping up until a couple of minutes ago. What's up?"

"What makes you think I'm not just calling to check up on you?"

"Spare me," she replied. It's... three a.m. This is a bit ridiculous even for you. "

"I... I need a favor, Sunny."

"Oh. Don't tell me, finally got fed up with that slut Shari. Came to your senses and popped her?"

Tom sighed. "No. And she left me a week ago anyway."

"Good. You can do better."

Tom's mouth turned into a smirk. "You think?"

"Yep, definitely. Anyway, how can your little sister help you at three oh two in the morning and it doesn't involve moving a dead stripper?"

"I need a gun. Thought you might be able to get me one. Nothing fancy. Simple pistol and enough ammunition to make a difference."

The camera turned on. Yeah, she'd dyed it purple. "Hold on. You working again?"

Tom frowned. "Maybe. Don't know. Got an offer on a line of work. Not sure it's the kind of thing I want to get into."

Sunny frowned back at him. "This isn't Defiant Strategy related, is it? I heard they went tits up, but you never can tell with some of these private contractors."

"No, it's not them. At least I don't think it is." Tom reached his right hand to touch his left arm. The metal felt cold under his fingers. "Freelancers though, used to work for them."

"And?" Sunny asked.

"O'Dell is the one putting together the team. Sent a guy named Shaman to see me about it."

"You think it's legit?"

Tom laughed, harsh and bitter. He didn't like how it sounded in his own ears. "Sam O'Dell involved in something legitimate? I doubt it. A better question is how much of myself I'll end up having to leave behind this time if I take him up on the offer."

"So walk away."

"The money though…"

"Yeah, yeah I get you. When do you need to give an answer by?"

"Friday."

"All right. I'll see what I can do about a gun for you. In the meantime, I'll do some sniffing around, see what I can get on O'Dell and company. Maybe get a line on what you are about to step into."

"I could walk away," Tom responded.

"Heh. Right. Anyway, I need to get some shut-eye. I'm supposed to go to brunch with Paula tomorrow morning."

"Ah. That your new girl?"

"If by new girl you mean the same girl I've been seeing the past six months, then yeah, it's the new girl."

Tom winced. "Sorry."

Sunny stifled a yawn. "Is okay. But seriously, this princess needs her beauty sleep. Night, Tom."

"G'night Sunny."

FOUR

Tom walked down streets slick with recent rain, a messenger bag slung across his chest. He breathed shallow, keeping his air mask up to filter out the worst of the toxins, but it never seemed to help with the smell, the reek of garbage piled against walls waiting for the latest sanitation strike to end. Tom wondered how long before it would be before that was automated as well.

The sun was still a few hours away, but the streets were lit well enough for his purposes. The City never really slept anyway. A stray cat paused on its way to stare at him before slinking off into the darkness. LED lights blinked on and off with no apparent pattern. He wondered if mute denizens were signaling to each other, warning people that a stranger was in their midst.

Tom kept his hands buried in his pockets, and his thick green-grey coat covered his arms and hid the majority of his bulk. He blinked, bringing up the address Sunny had provided into his overlay. He superimposed a map over his vision, followed the blinking yellow arrow to his destination.

He slipped into an alley, immediately felt eyes boring into his back. He shook his right hand out of his pocket, kept his metal one buried in his jacket. A figure stepped out from behind a dumpster, and he heard the scrape of boots on asphalt behind him. The figure in front of him had his head shaved, electrical circuitry tattooed on the sides of his head in day-glo orange. Light gleamed off the serrated blade in his hand, and his one good eye wept onto his cheek. Tom could hear the jangle of a chain being let out behind him.

"Just passing through," Tom said, holding his flesh and blood hand up and open, palm out. "Not looking for trouble."

Tom heard the person behind him giggle. "Not looking for trouble, he says." The one in front cut the air with his knife. "Must be a shame that trouble found you."

"Cough up the bag," the one with the knife said. He wrinkled his nose. "And the jacket."

"Hey, he's got nice boots. Get those too."

Tom shook his head. "Are you sure you want to go down this road?"

"You heard me, bag and jacket. I'd hate to get blood on my new jacket."

"And the boots!" the high-pitched voice added.

"Yeah, yeah, boots too."

Tom shrugged his shoulders. "Last chance," he warned, his cybernetic hand balling into a fist in his pocket. He felt the artificial muscle tense, felt his heart beat increase. He blinked, getting rid of the overlay and shifted his feet slightly.

The knife came in first. Tom exploded into action, his metal fist striking the blade and sending it spinning through the air. He heard it hit an alley wall. The chain struck him across the back, but his reinforced jacket took the worst of it. He stumbled from the blow, but gothis feet back under him. He launched a rear kick, catching the second attacker in the knee. He heard it snap under the blow, heard the howl of pain. Tom stepped in and kicked hard at the second attackers chin.

Turning around, he caught a solid blow to his chin from the knife wielder. He rocked back on his feet, and when the first attacker tried to follow-up with a blow to Tom's midsection, he blocked it with his metal arm. The attacker's arm broke like a dry stick and he cried out for a moment before Tom grabbed him by the hair and slammed him into the dumpster.

Tom rubbed his chin and kicked the chain away.

"Amateurs," he muttered, shaking his head and rubbing his jaw. He brought the map back up, checked where he was. He walked down another twisting, cramped alleyway, stopping in front of a security door. A lone camera stared down, unblinking, over the steel door. Tom pressed the buzzer.

"You the guy daylight20 recommended?" the intercom squawked.

Tom blinked, then remembered that was Sunny's hacker nom de plume. "Yeah, she said you could set me up."

"How do I know it's you?"

Tom sighed through his mask and held up his left arm, pulling the jacket back to reveal the laced titanium gleaming dull in the half-light of the city before daybreak.

"Yeah, guess that'll do for an invitation. Come on in."

The door buzzed open, and Tom walked down a steep flight of concrete stairs illuminated by a single bare bulb. His eyes adjusted to the sudden brightness. The door clicked shut behind him, and he was faced with a second security door and a second camera. He pulled off his filtration mask.

"You really daylight20's brother?" a second intercom box squawked at him.

Tom resisted the urge to roll his eyes. "Yeah. Say, those weren't your goons out in the alley were they?"

"Who, those assholes? Nah. I gotta say I got a thrill from watching you kick the shit out of them though. They keep smashing my cameras."

Tom forced a smile. "Not a problem."

The door buzzed and Tom walked through.

Sitting behind thick security glass, a balding man sat, peering through thick, scratched glasses at Tom. "So you're here about the gun?"

Tom nodded. "I sure as shit didn't come for the décor."

"Watching how you handled yourself though, makes me wonder why you even want a gun."

Tom's smile vanished. "What do you care so long as I can pay?

The old man cackled and turned to his workbench. "I like you, son. Come here. I cobbled together something for you."

Tom looked through the security glass. On the other side was a long work bench, along with a complete machinist's shop. A partially put together machinegun lay on top of one table, on another, bullets in various stages of assemble lay scattered around. The smell of cordite filled the air, and the distinct smell of burning metal.

"You do all your own work in house?"

"Be a fool if I didn't. All those corporations out there, with their own guns, handing them out to their dogs. Putting leashes on them is what they do. They know when any of those guns is fired and at what."

The old man moved his chair over to one side, which was when Tom realized he was missing his legs at the knees. "But there's enough metal and old weapons floating around out there that I've got enough raw materials to keep me busy for the next twenty years."

"How do you get the material though?"

The man wheeled his chair to another table. On it, a partly disassembled wheel drone lay, most of its internal workings sprawled out over the surface. "Send these little buggers out every few days.

They bring me back things. Most of its junk, but some of it's useable. I take it part, machine it, put it back together into something new."

Tom nodded. "Yeah. So about that gun?"

"What'd you get me?"

Tom opened the messenger bag, placed a brown wrapped package into a rotating glass partition. The old man spun it around, grabbed the package and tore into it. He looked up and smiled, all gap toothed and rotten.

"Heh, she does know what I like," he said, holding up a bottle filled with a translucent liquid that shimmered in the light. He pulled a pistol out from under the table, a black boxy looking weapon. A sight was mounted on top of it, with a LED flashlight mounted under the barrel. He added six clips of ammunition, and another five boxes of the same next to that.

"As promised. 10mm bullets. You won't find this beauty registered anywhere. Nice flat black finish, so it won't gleam in the light. Built in suppressor. People'll still hear you when you fire it, but you shouldn't need to wear earplugs with this darling."

"I'm familiar with how suppressors work," Tom said.

"You were in the service?"

Tom shook his head. He hefted the gun. It was lighter than he thought it would be otherwise. "Carbon fiber?"

"And aluminum. Barrel's an alloy. You were private corp?"

Tom shrugged and put the gun, magazines and bullets into his bag. "Defiant Strategy."

"Never heard of them."

"They didn't operate much state side. Saw some action down in LatAm."

"That where you pick up that souvenir?" the old man asked, pointing at Tom's arm.

"Yeah."

The old man smiled. He reached under the table again, placed a small black knife on the table, along with a sheath for it. "Goes around your ankle," he said. "From one vet to another." He tapped the stumps where his legs ended.

"I didn't really-"

The old man waved a dismissive hand. "You fought. You sacrificed. Probably so someone a lot richer than you would see his stock portfolio shift a point in the right direction. Take it and don't insult me by refusing."

"All right. Thanks-" Tom realized he didn't know the old man's name.

The man smiled, wrinkles crinkling around his eyes. "Hank. Hope to do business with you again, Tom."

"Likewise."

Tom exited the weapon smith and back into the early morning light of the city, the sun creeping up over the horizon, beams of light streaming between the buildings. There was no sign of the two attackers. Slipping on his filtration mask, Tom queued his map for a nearby diner and pulled out the card Shaman had given him.

He blinked his eyes and started walking. The phone in his head dialed Shaman's number.

"Hello Tom."

"You knew it was me?"

"You're the only one who has this number that I couldn't identify."

Tom let that sit for a bit, let it swirl around in his head and settle in his gut. "I'll meet with Sam."

"Not good enough. We need a commitment on this, Tom. Half-assing it won't cut it."

"You expect me to sign up blind? No dice. Tell O'Dell we have a meeting, and I get enough of the details to make an informed decision. Understand?"

There was a brief pause on the other end. "Yeah, Sam says that's reasonable. Let me get you an address."

"No. I'll tell you where I want to meet."

"You don't trust us?" Shaman sounded hurt.

"I trust you as much as I trust anyone, Shaman. I'll send the address over along with a time. It'll be tonight. That's non-negotiable, by the way."

"He'll be there."

Tom heard the phone click, leaving him alone. He looked up at the pollution blue of the city sky, forced his flesh and blood hand to unclench. He walked into the diner, took off his mask, and ordered a coffee. The shaking stopped by the time he finished his first cup.

FIVE

Tom walked through the mall at seven o'clock. Most of the store fronts sat empty, and the few that were still open were closing up shop. A few restaurants and the like were still open, people walking back and forth, keeping their eyes down and their conversations hushed. Smart ads blared out from cracked screens, and there was the constant whir of delivery drones in the space above the shoppers.

Tom leaned against a wall, fingered the cigarettes in his pocket. The mall was strictly no smoking, and he didn't want any hassle from the rent-a-cops walking their beat.

O'Dell didn't try to hide as he made his way through the crowd toward Tom, cutting like a shark among minnows. The civvies gave him a wide berth, even if he wasn't visibly armed. The way he carried himself though… it made Tom think of a wolf he'd seen once. In captivity, of course, but the way it stalked and prowled around, the way its eyes took in the world. There was something of the apex predator to O'Dell. Tom figured that's what had made him agree all those years ago. That and the chance to get out of prison.

Five years hadn't changed O'Dell. He still sported the handlebar moustache, still had a face like carved slate. He didn't smile when he spotted Tom, but his eyes sparkled in the same way they did when he was coming up with a plan. He was dressed simply, a nice suit, button down shirt but no tie. Tom was fairly sure he spotted a bulge under his arm, probably something low caliber.

"Tom."

"Sam."

"Been a while."

"Five years, sir."

"Yeah, it has been hasn't it? See they got you a new arm. Couldn't save the old one?"

Tom looked down at his hand, opened and closed it slowly, watching the fibers ben and stretch. "No. Surprised you didn't come and see me after."

Sam shrugged. "Wasn't really a choice. After the Caracas fiasco, they deployed us back out again. You were still in post-op when they had us dust off. All we knew was that you'd come through okay."

Tom glanced down at his arm again. "Mostly."

Sam nodded. "Yeah. Surprised they gave you one of those. Most people these days are going with organic replacements."

Tom allowed himself a small smile. "It was a provision in my contract when I signed up. Took off a fraction of my pay, put it into a separate account. I'd picked this out before we even left the City. Thought you would have known that, seeing as how you were my recruiting officer."

Sam chuckled. "I left the paperwork to the lawyers. All I cared about was getting you to sign on the dotted line. Good for you though."

Tom shrugged. "Not sure how smart it was. Most people don't want to hire someone sporting something like this. Artificial eyes or a direct neural link? Yeah, those are socially acceptable." He raises his hand, turns it around in front of him. "This, not so much."

Sam frowned. "So why not get a covering for it? I know I've seen some pretty realistic ones out there."

Tom stuck his hand back in his jacket pocket. "You know how well they hold up to regular wear and tear? Yeah, if I was working some cush desk job and living in a neighborhood where I wasn't worried about getting into a fight once a week, then yeah, I'd think about it. As it is I'd be dropping a couple of grand on something that would get shredded in a month. Not worth it."

"Yeah, guess I can see that," Sam said.

"Anyway, I don't think you wanted to see me just so you could admire the new hardware."

"Shaman tell you I had a job for you?"

Tom nodded. He watched as a security guard walked by, his hand on his stun gun as he eyed Sam and Tom. Tom gave a brief shake of his head, and the guard decided he wasn't all that curious. They weren't bothering anyone, just two men having a conversation. Not blocking pedestrian traffic. Not blocking an entrance into a store or restaurant. Only a couple of hard men looking like they might take it amiss if there conversation were suddenly interrupted.

"He didn't say any more than that, did he?" Sam followed up.

"Only that it was a limited engagement and that I was your first choice. That, and Defiant Strategy wasn't bankrolling you. So what crime are you up to, Sam?"

Sam winced and placed a hand over his heart. "Crime? Me?" He laughed. "Yeah, I'll admit what I'm proposing isn't legitimate. There's something we've been contracted to steal. It isn't anything we'd be able to move on our own, some sort of chemical compound or something. Egghead shit, really. But eggheads can't do what we can."

"You'll break Ju-Won's heart talking like that," Tom said. "He's in on this?"

Sam nodded. "We get you on board and it'll be the whole crew."

"I'm surprised you all stuck together after Defiant went down."

Sam shook his head. "Wasn't like that. We all went our separate ways after Defiant collapsed. Took a couple of years off. Tried living like normal people." He scratched his cheek, his eyes locked on Tom. "Guess none of us found it agreeable. So are you in?"

"Who's the target?" Tom asked.

"Kandex. You know them?"

"Nope."

"So what does it matter?"

"Guess it doesn't. When are you looking to make your move?"

"Two days from now." Same passed a scrap of paper to Tom with GPS coordinates on it. "You need to be here in three hours if you're in. Bring enough clothes for a few days."

"What about weapons?"

"I've provided, but feel free to bring your own. I'm not anticipating a fire fight though if that's what you're worried about."

Tom wrinkled his nose but nodded. "All right. I'll see you at the spot. Three hours, right?"

Sam nodded. "Give or take. We've got some prep work to do, and we need to work you into the plan."

"Thought Shaman said there was a back-up in case I said no."

Sam smiled. "Maybe. I wanted someone local to the area. We tossed around a few ideas, and your name came up." He turned and walked away, trying and failing to disappear into the crowd, his military bearing too ingrained to hide. Tom thought he spotted a figure move near one of the skylights, but put it down to being paranoid.

He shoved his hands back in his pockets, fingers itching for a cigarette. He stepped out into the night air of the city, nearly gagged on the sulfurous smell before he got his filtration mask back on. He dialed Sunny as he walked back toward his apartment. She answered, but kept the video off.

"Hey, bro."

"You find anything out about what Sam might be up to?"

"Nada. Hey, you meet with him yet?"

"Yeah, I agreed to the job. Sounds like it's a simple snatch and grab. Some company named Kandex, know anything about it? Sounds like they might be a petrochem company. Sounds like we might be hitting their Research and Development department in two days."

"Name doesn't really ring a bell, but I don't watch the stock market. Doesn't mean I can't find out a few details though. Who does he have on the gig?"

"He said he's got the whole crew back together."

"Including Rayen? I remember that picture you had of all of you. Right before the Caracas job, right? She's cute."

"Focus Sunny."

She laughed. "Where are you meeting up with the old crew?"

Tom read off the GPS coordinates.

"You people. Can't you ever just have an address?"

Tom chuckled. "You never were in Venezuela. GPS was often the best we could do. Otherwise it would be 'Yeah, we'll be over at the burned out gas station where the church burned down five years ago.' Old habits die hard."

"Anyway, I've got an address for you. Looks like it's a warehouse. Currently empty, but formerly owned by, hey, get this Defiant Strategy."

"Who owns it now?" Tom took a circuitous walk back toward his apartment.

"One S. O'Dell."

"Huh. He's been planning this for a while now, hasn't he?"

"Hard to tell, but he's owned it for three years now. So… maybe."

"Maybe?" Tom slowed down, studied an empty storefront for a bit. He tried to tell if anyone was following him, but the streets were still crowded enough that it was hard to tell. Of course, Ju-Won could be flying a drone a mile up and tracking him and he'd have no good way of knowing.

"I can think lots of reasons to own a warehouse. All empty. Just waiting to be filled with knickknacks and electronics and about fifty monitors." Sunny trailed off, lost in a daydream of owning that much space.

"I've seen your apartment, Sunny. If you had that much space, we'd never see you again."

"And it would be glorious! Ahem. Yes. So that's all I could find in a short period of time. Oh, and you should know there's someone in your apartment."

"Wait, what?" Tom was a block from his apartment. He resisted the urge to draw his pistol, but its weight on his hip was less reassuring than he might have liked.

"Someone tripped the alarm in your apartment. I thought you should know."

"Front door or window?"

"Hmm, oh they came through the front door."

"You know, you could have said something earlier, Sunny." Tom walked around to the side of his building. The fire escape looked precarious, decades of neglect leaving it a rusted wreck. He was reasonably sure it would still hold though.

"Yeah, but where's the fun in that?" she asked. "Try not to get killed. You're my favorite brother."

"I'm your only brother," Tom growled through clenched teeth. "Anyway, it's probably Shari."

"Didn't you change the locks the last time you broke up?"

"And the security codes. That's why she had to break in."

"Okay, anyway. I'll get back to you on the Kandex info I dig up."

"Bye Sunny."

"Bye."

Tom reached up and grabbed the chain some helpful soul had hooked to the fire escape ladder. As he climbed up, he drew his pistol and tried to quiet the hammering in his chest. He sent a silent code from the phone in his head to the window in his kitchen, disengaging the lock. He pushed it open, wincing at the way the warped wood protested. He slid inside the room in time for the light to switch on.

Two figures stood in his room, both dressed casually in button down shirts and black pants. Both wore the dark glasses and had the kind of haircuts Tom always associated with corporate security.

"You're not Shari," he said. He kept his gun pointed down and his finger off the trigger.

"Mr. Costigan?"

Tom worked his tongue around his teeth, forced the bile back down into his throat. "Could be."

"This is his apartment, isn't it?"

"That's what I hear. How do I know it doesn't belong to one of you?"

The one on the right's smile disappeared as quick as it appeared, making Tom wonder if the man's mouth moved at all. "Please Mr. Costigan. Don't treat us like idiots, and we'll try to show you the same courtesy."

"All right. So who are you?" Tom peeled off his filtration mask and shut the window to keep the worst of the night smog out.

"We represent Kandex. Have you heard of us?"

Tom shook his head. "Can't say I have."

"Kandex is a small outfit. We try to stay out of the press, other than trade journals. We're focused mostly on research and development, though we do have a few patents out there in the world."

"Huh. Interesting. Not sure what any of that has to do with me however." Tom put his gun down on the kitchen counter, but still close enough he'd be able to grab it if things went sideways.

"Are you familiar with a man named Samuel O'Dell?"

"Yeah, I know Sam. We worked together at Defiant Strategy. Haven't seen him, in, oh about five years or so. Why?"

"We've received intelligence that Mr. O'Dell might be engaged in a criminal enterprise targeting Kandex resources. We think he might be trying to reach out to former associates."

"Is that so?" Tom felt his heart pounding in his chest, tried to keep his breathing regular. "Like I said, I haven't seen him."

One of the agents reached into his jacket pocket. Tom kept himself still, resisting the urge to grab his gun. He relaxed when the agent pulled out a card, held it out for Tom to take. It was a simple white card, a number printed in black on it. No corporate logo. No name.

"If you did hear anything, and passed that information along, there'd be a reward in it for such an upstanding citizen. Of course, we are going to be going after Mr. O'Dell with extreme prejudice, along with whomever is working with him."

Tom reached out and took the card, pinching it between two calloused fingers. "Yeah, I'll be sure to call. But like I said, I haven't talked to him in years."

The agents both nodded. "He might have sent someone else to talk to you. Maybe a former comrade?" the second agent asked.

Tom shook his head. "Haven't talked to anyone from those days for a long, long time. If I do, you'll be the first to know."

The two agents looked at each other and came to a silent understanding. "All right," the second agent said. "Be sure to call us though. You don't want to get caught on the wrong side of this."

"Got it. Now, if that's all, kindly get the fuck out of my apartment. I've had a long day and would like to get some sleep."

"Good night, Mr. Costigan."

The two men exited Tom's apartment, and he closed the door behind them. He wasn't sure how they'd gotten in, but they hadn't damaged the lock. After securing it, he packed a bag as he head dialed Sunny.

"What's up?" Sunny kept her video feed off. Tom figured she had someone over.

"Kandex decided to pay me a visit. Well, a couple of their goons anyway."

"Well, fuck."

"Exactly."

"They say what they wanted?"

"Wanted to know if Sam had been on touch with me."

"Yeah?"

"Yeah. Seems they know Sam is up to something, but they aren't sure what. They left me a card to get in touch with them." Tom took the card out of his pocket. He took a snap shot of it with his cyber eyes, then set it aflame in the kitchen sink.

"So what are you going to do?"

"Going to see Sam and company. I don't like being threatened."

"Do you think you can trust Sam?"

Tom laughed. "Fuck no. But I can trust Sam to work toward his own self-interest. These corporate assholes? Fuck them."

Tom slung his duffel bag over his shoulder, grabbed his gun from the kitchen and made sure he had his messenger bag with his extra ammunition packed and ready. He opened a second line in his head and called for a cab. He closed it, went back to Sunny. "You find anything else out?"

"Not yet," Sunny said. "Kandex has a bunch of articles published in journals about their research efforts. Seems to be a lot about neurochemical interactions and how to influence them. Very technical. Very boring."

"That lines up with what Sam said, then, that we're doing this job on behalf of someone else."

"I guess. I don't know. Why bring you in to a simple theft? No offense, Tom, but you aren't exactly what I would call Mr. Subtle."

"Thanks. I don't know. But it's got to pay better than washing dishes, right?"

"Yeah, sure. Just don't get shot, all right?"

"I'll do my best."

"Night, Tom."

"Night."

Tom checked the lock and the alarm on his door one last time, then ducked out the fire escape. He checked the skies, but if there were any drones out there spying on him they were too high up and it was too dark to make them out. He walked the three blocks where he'd told the cab to meet him. It was one of the old gypsy style cabs, reeking of incense on the inside. Tom handed the driver a scrap of paper with the intersection he wanted to get dropped off at. He settled back in the car, listening to the Romanian punk rock playing at a low volume. He closed his eyes for a moment, then opened them as soon as the cab stopped.

The driver raised an eyebrow when Tom paid him double what the fare was worth and in cash, but bid him a good night. Tom shouldered his bag and walked the six blocks to the warehouse, the streets empty in this part of the city except for the occasional stray dog. Even the ever present hum of drones was missing. Tom saw the warehouse Sam had given him the coordinates to, saw Ju-Won standing outside, smoking a cigarette. He held a shotgun by the stock and his face brightened into a smile when he saw Tom approach.

"Damn, Rayen's going to be pissed when she sees you?"

Tom blinked. "What? Why?"

"She bet you wouldn't show up. I was the only one that took her up on it. See you got some new hardware," he said, pointing to Tom's metal hand.

Tom nodded. He wasn't the only one. Ju-Won had shaved his head, and he saw a direct neural interface been implanted above the hacker's left ear. "How've you been?"

Ju-Won shrugged. "Bored. Last few years have been pretty slow since Defiant folded."

"I understand you're the one that tracked me down?"

"Oh don't look at me like that. You weren't all that hard to track down, if you knew where to look."

Tom shrugged. "Thought I'd covered my tracks pretty well."

The hacker sniffed. "You went back to your old neighborhood, started falling back into your old patterns. Took me about three months to put enough of a pattern together where I could have Shaman find you. It was still a pretty close thing, given our time line."

Tom blinked. "Oh. So I guess Sam's been planning this for a while then."

"Yeah, you could say that."

"Everyone else inside?"

"Yep, just us two," Ju-Won replied. "Let's go say hi."

Ju-Won opened the door to the warehouse and ushered Tom in. Sam had been busy, a full staging area arranged inside. Two sedan cars were parked, their hoods up, mechanic lights shining down into their interiors. Rayen was bent over one of the engines, lifted her grease stained face long enough to wave to Tom. Anatoliy sat at a work bench, hand busy stripping weapons down, checking them, and putting them back together. The three long tables around him were covered with guns, parts, and ammunition. "Tom!" he called out, and Tom smiled back. The Ukrainian looked bigger than Tom remembered, older too. He had to guess that he looked older as well.

Shaman and O'Dell were standing over by a separate table, blue prints spread out across the table. Shaman saw Tom first and nudged O'Dell.

"Tom, glad you decided to join us," Sam said, extending his hand. Tom took it, felt Sam's firm grip.

"Yes, sir, seemed like it wasn't the sort of thing to let pass me by."

Sam smiled. "Good. We have most of the other bases covered. Rayen's handling our wheels. Shaman will be covering us here." Sam stabbed down with his finger at a point on the map. "Ju-Won is going to be running drone coverage and hacking the door combinations once we are inside."

Tom looked down at the plans. "You want to hit it during daylight?"

"The entire place goes on full lockdown at 8:00 pm," Shaman explained. "We don't have any choice but to hit it during the day."

"And no chance of trying to hit it while in transport?"

Shaman and Sam shared a long look. "We tried that already," Sam said by way of explanation. "That's why it is there now."

"Anatoliy will be heavy weapons, as per usual. Tom, I need you with me once we're inside. We'll be covering Ju-Won and handling any internal security measures."

Tom worked his tongue around his teeth. "So what are we stealing?"

Sam looked hard at Tom. "Thought I told you. A chemical compound."

"And some research notes," Ju-Won chimed in.

"Yeah. How worried should we be if the chemical leaks? Am I going to be glowing in the dark? Growing a third eye? Worrying about my dick falling off?"

Sam shrugged. "No idea, but we're being paid well enough to assume that risk. If you want out though…" He pointed to the door.

Tom took a deep breath. "No, I'm in."

Sam placed a hand on Tom's shoulder. "Good. Now here's the plan."

SIX

Tom hit the ground at a run, Rayen barely slowing down as he, Ju-Won, Anatoliy and Sam piled out. The two security guards at the gate tried to get their guns up in time, but Sam brought his suppressed assault rifle up and fired two quick bursts.

"They're going to know something's up," Tom said.

"You've got movement in the building folks," Shaman's voice crackled in Tom's earpiece.

Ju-Won dropped the hard case he was carrying. It looked like nothing so much as an overlarge suitcase. He popped it open, unfolding two hawk-sized drones into the air. They quickly lifted up, began their air patrol of the area. Anatoliy entered the reception area, his machinegun already mounted on a shoulder harness.

"Everyone get down and no one will be hurt!" The big man's voice echoed throughout the area. The receptionist, a young man with a bare hint of fuzz on his face, slowly got to the ground behind the desk. "No, get out here, get on the ground. Tom?"

"I got him," Tom replied, zip-tieing the man's hands. The reception area was otherwise empty.

A woman came through the door, her eyes fixed on a clipboard. "Kevin, could you- Wait, what's going on?"

Tom rushed her, knocking her to the ground. As he secured her wrists, he whispered in her ear, "Stay down and stay quiet. We aren't here to hurt anyone, understand?"

Tom and Sam dragged the security guards into the reception area. Kevin and the woman averted their eyes, the woman gasping in short sharp breaths to keep from crying out. Ju-Won secured the front door, making sure it was locked. Sam covered the door going further into the office. Anatoliy busied himself with setting up his machine gun on the reception desk, using it to create an impromptu nest.

"How are we doing Ju-Won?" Sam asked.

"So far so good," the hacker declared. "No signs of trouble yet. The drones aren't picking anything up either, but they've knocked out Kandex's security drones in the perimeter. Figure the real police will be showing up in the next ten to fifteen."

"Shaman?"

"You've got movement on the upper floors. Looks like in-house security is on to you. Huh. Looks like they are taking cover now. Must be because some asshole with a sniper rifle drilled two of them and they have no idea where the shots are coming from."

"That's why we keep you around," Sam responded. "Ready Tom?"

Tom moved into the office space, keeping a low stance. He passed several workers, already on the ground, their fingers laced together at the back of their heads. Probably not the first time they'd seen a hostile armed team during their work day. Some of them might even think it was a standard security drill.

Tom rounded a corner and immediately jumped back, automatic fire stitching through the cubicle. Tom returned fire, was rewarded with the sound of a curse cut short. He got down on his stomach, fetched a small mirror from the combat webbing he wore, and used it to peer around the corner.

"One down. There are still two gunmen over there."

"Think you can get them?"

Tom smiled, angled his gun using the mirror, and sent a burst of automatic fire through the partitions. The two of them rounded the corner, checked the bodies.

"I'm not seeing any other office workers," Tom commented.

"Probably headed to their panic room," Sam replied. "Shaman, any eyes on the security teams?"

"Not at the moment. They finally figured they should stay back from the windows."

"Ju-Won?"

"Offsite security is inbound. Looks like they are taking an aerial approach."

"Anything your drones can do about it?"

"That's a negative. Looks like an armored VTOL craft. I'd be just as well throwing rocks at it."

"Understood, let's hustle people."

Tom entered the cubicle farm. The workers had left their workstations in obvious haste, email accounts and spreadsheets still open on their screens. He shook his head. He'd figured everyone would have switched over to virtual reality interfaces or direct neural links like Ju-Won. He guessed not every wage slave could make that kind of investment. He rounded a corner, got rocked back when he felt like he'd been kicked in the chest. He dropped back, stunned, realized he'd been shot. Lucky, his vest stopped the bullet. More bullets followed, tearing through the cubicle walls like tissue paper.

"I think we found the security team," he gasped to Sam.

"You all right?"

"Yeah, the vest stopped it."

"Good. Any idea how many?"

Tom shrugged. "Figure a standard response team. Four people or so."

"See any civvies?"

Tom shook his head. "Think they all cleared out."

"All right. Anatoliy, how are you doing?"

"Everything is copacetic. No news is good news, yes?"

"Yeah, maybe," Sam replied. "Shaman?"

"All quiet here, though there's a lot of local chatter. Seems you guys kicked the hornet's nest on this one. Only good news is local police are being told to hold back. Looks like Kandex is taking this kind of personal."

Sam pulled a grenade off his webbing. "Flash bang," he mouthed to Tom. Tom nodded in reply, tucked his head back and made sure to cover his ears with his arms. He heard it go off, and then he was going around the corner. He fired his submachinegun in controlled bursts. The security team, dazed and blinded by the flashbang, didn't stand a chance. They'd been guarding a security door with a keycard entry in their way.

Tom consulted the blueprint he'd taken a snapshot of with his cybereye. "Yeah, this is the way we want to go," he confirmed.

"Ju-Won?" Sam called.

"Don't need him," Tom said. He searched one of the downed guards, pulled free a security card. He tapped it against the door lock and the light switched from red to green.

"Amateurs," Sam chuckled. "Let's go. Downstairs, right?"

"Yeah."

Tom took point as they maneuvered into the stairwell, flipping on the LED light on his gun. The building had switched over to emergency lighting, and they could hear the siren wail echoing off the concrete. At the bottom of the stairs was another lock, this one designed for a retinal scan and thumbprint.

"I've got this," Ju-Won confirmed. He opened his messenger bag. First he pried off the plastic casing, exposing the electronics underneath. He attached a device to the exposed wires, connected them to the direct neural port implanted above his right ear.

"Is that such a good idea?" Tom asked. "I've heard some of these corps have pretty intense security, enough to fry your brain if you aren't careful."

Ju-Won didn't answer.

"Ju-Won?" Tom asked.

"Leave him be," Sam cautioned. He kept up a watch near the bottom of the stairs, gun at the ready in case anyone tried to come up behind them. "He's in there, which means he can't afford to pay attention to you to. Let him work."

"Fine." As Tom waited, he felt the pain radiating through his chest where he'd been shot, and he slumped against the wall. His breathing came fast and shallow and he blinked his eyes. He remembered getting shot, the fact catching up to him now that the endorphins were fading.

"Tom? You all right?"

Tom shook his head, tried to wave Sam away. Sam pulled Tom's hands away from his chest, saw the bullet hole. "Damn son, looks like you got tagged." Sam pulled something from his webbing, tore it open with his teeth and slapped it against Tom's neck. The pain stared to fade almost instantly, and Tom found the darkness receding.

"Getting shot is no joke."

"You don't say," Tom gasped. "Seems I make a habit of it when I'm on mission with you."

The door clicked open, and Ju-Won blinked. "Sorry Tom, did you say something?" he asked with a grin.

"Never mind." Tom went through the door first. Standing in front of him was an older scientist, gray hair sticking up at odd angles. He peered at Tom through thick glasses, his shaking hands holding a gun far too large for his frame.

"You won't get any further than this," he said. "I don't know who hired you, but this is my life work. You can't just-"

He was cut short with a shot from Sam's gun, the bullet entering his skull between his eyes and blowing the back of his head wide open.

"Why'd you do that?" Ju-Won asked. "He could have told us what we were looking for."

"We didn't have time for a lengthy conversation," Sam countered. He pointed to a black box about the size of a toaster oven. "That's the

31

computer. Think you can get in and download what we need?"

Ju-Won nodded. "I'm on it." He fished in his bag for a moment before pulling out an external drive. Hurrying over, he connected it to the computer. "What exactly am I looking for?"

"Anything related to Project Prometheus," Sam said. "Particularly we need chemical composition and any procedures for administration."

"Administration?" Tom asked. "What the hell is this stuff?"

Sam shrugged. "No idea. Figured we were getting paid enough I didn't have to ask. Start looking for the compound."

Tom looked around. They were surrounded by three glass enclosed labs. He walked over to one, saw that it needed a key card as well. "Dead guy there have a key card on him?" Tom asked.

"Why yes he does," Sam confirmed. He pulled it off the scientist's lab coat, swiped it across the access for Tom. He walked in. Inside, it reeked of antiseptic and bleach. Esoteric measuring equipment Tom couldn't even begin to guess the names of were arrayed meticulously on the lab tables. Along one wall, cages of rats chittered nervously to each other. He opened a fridge, saw a small steel case. A white label across it labeled it as Project Prometheus.

"Think I got it," Tom said.

Sam came over, pulled a device out of his pocket.

"What's that?"

"Our way of making sure," Sam said. He checked the case over. "Huh."

"What's wrong?"

"What do you make of that?" he asked, pointing to a small raised button on the bottom of the case.

"Triggering device?"

"Yeah." Sam pulled a small knife from his pocket, slid it along the seam of the case.

"Gentlemen, you are going to want to hurry up," Shaman said. "The VTOL just landed and it looks like a full response team is deploying. Oh joy, they brought counter-snipers."

"Is your position compromised?" Sam asked, pausing in opening the case.

"Not yet, but I'm not going to be able to do much good from up here. Heading to cover the extraction point."

"Understood. Anatoliy?"

"I heard," the big man replied. "Holding position for now. What's your timeline?"

Tom looked over at Ju-Won who was still unresponsive, locked away into the software, looking for the data they required. "No idea." Sam went back to work on the case. "Heh. Simple triggering mechanism. You don't hold the trigger down, and the whole case goes up. Thermite, probably. Crude, but effective." He popped the case open. Inside were three vials of a mercurial looking substance along with three syringes.

"That's it?" Tom asked.

Sam took out one of the vials, placed it in a scanner. All the lights turned green, and he smiled wide. "That's it. Ju-Won?"

The hacker shook himself, unplugged the cable from his head. "Yeah, I'm done here. You get the package?"

Sam took the vials, put them into a padded pouch in his hip bag. "We're good."

"Anatoliy?"

"Not good, gentlemen. We need to go now. Pulling back to the exit."

"Got that," Sam confirmed.

"Shaman?"

"All set. They haven't moved to cover our exit yet."

"Good. Rayen?"

"Waiting for the word."

Sam smiled at Tom and Ju-Won. "Time to go."

They came out into the stairway. Out of the lab, they could hear the staccato reports of gunfire echoing through the building. They hurried, Tom following the blueprint plan and leading the way. They stumbled over a body, one arm missing, and a second, slumped against a bloody wall. The trio emerged into an office area. Anatoliy was engaged with the remaining members of the security force, his machine gun flinging out a storm of lead. The office furniture looked like a giant had picked it up and chewed on it for a while. The first the security team knew they were in trouble was when turned around to see their partner slumped over, their throat cut by Tom's knife. The guard opened his mouth to warn the others, but that's when Ju-Won blew the front of his face off with his shotgun. The others turned, startled, and that's when Anatoliy brought his big gun around to bear. Tom, Sam, and Ju-Won kept back, trying to keep the supporting walls between themselves and the big Ukrainian as possible.

"All clear," he called out.

"Let's go, let's go, let's go," Sam called, and they hurried for the back door to the alley. "Rayen, we are on our way. Shaman?"

"Still clear."

Anatoliy was the first through the door, followed by Sam, each covering a different approach on the alley. Tom followed, and as he got to the entrance, Rayen pulled up in the van, the doors on the side automatically opening. Tom turned to cover the hallway from where they'd just come from, but only in time to see Ju-Won stumble, followed by the sharp report of a gun. The hacker got back to his feet and stumbled into the van as Tom returned fire.

"Shit, they got Ju-Won," Tom called out, grabbing the medical kit they had stashed in the van. The bullet had punched through the bullet proof vest completely. He got a compress on it, Ju-Won's hands feebly clutching at his clothes.

"T-tom," he spluttered, blood on his lips.

Anatoliy turned the machine gun on the hallway and let loose with a stream of suppressing fire as Sam got into the van. "Let's go Anatoliy!" Sam yelled as he strapped himself in. The big man stepped back, ducking low under the van's ceiling.

"Go, go, go!"

Rayen sped off at Sam's orders, Tom still trying to stop the bleeding.

"Hot shit, we did it!" Sam said, punching the roof. "Shaman, you clearing out?"

"Yeah, just deterring a couple of pursuers. I'll see you back at the safe house."

"Hear that, Ju-Won? We did it! And you were worried about a direct attack. Ju-Won?"

Tom met Sam's eyes and shook his head. He placed his hand over Ju-Won's eyes and closed him with the flat of his hand.

"What about the hard drive? It's intact, right?"

Tom wrinkled his nose, a heat building in his chest that threatened to explode, but he passed the bag over to Sam just the same. "Oh, good, the hard drive is fine."

"Yeah, good thing Ju-Won was there to catch the bullet, huh?"

Sam looked hard at Tom. Anatoliy looked everywhere but at the two of them. "He knew the risks. We accomplished the mission. That's what matters."

Tom sniffed and ran his tongue along his back teeth. "Yeah. I guess it is."

"Everything all right back there?" Rayen asked.

Tom leaned back and closed his eyes.

"Yeah, everything's going to be all right. It's still a six way split. I'll make sure Ju-Won's share gets to where he wanted it to go."

Tom opened his eyes to see Sam staring hard at him. "Look, I don't like the fact that he's dead either. But how much worse would it be if he was dead and we didn't get the data we were hired to retrieve? What then? What would his death mean then? Fuck. All."

Tom nodded. "Yeah, yeah. I get it." He shook his head. "Been a long night, and well, it's never easy, is it?"

Sam shrugged. "Never is, when it's one of your own."

SEVEN

Rayen took a circuitous route back to the safe house, careful to avoid breaking any traffic regulations on their way. When she pulled up into the loading area, Shaman was already there, leaning against his motorcycle. He blinked once when Anatoliy and Tom exited the van, carrying Ju-Won's lifeless body between them, then came over to help them.

"What went wrong?" he asked.

Sam shook his head. "Somebody on the other side got lucky. Or we got unlucky. It doesn't matter though, does it?"

"We get everything we wanted?"

"Yeah," Tom replied. "Except for Ju-Won." Shaman cleared off one of the tables, laid a tarp down, and Anatoliy and Tom deposited him on top of it with as much ceremony as they could muster.

Sam shot Tom a look. "I need to call our backers, let them know the job is done and arrange for the transfer." He looked around the warehouse. "Start breaking this down. I don't want anything left here that could be tracked back to us, understand?"

Anatoliy snorted. "Not our first rodeo, now is it?"

Tom cracked a smile. "Anatoliy, you've been practicing your idioms."

The big man shrugged. "It helps pass the time between jobs."

The two men started collecting weapons and ammunition, packing them into crates which then went into the two vans. Shaman worked collecting all of the intel. He'd found an empty steel drum and had started a fire, a fine grey smoke filling the air as he burned the documents.

Rayen checked over the vehicles again, an unlit cigarette hanging off her bottom lip. She caught Tom looking at her and winked at him before walking over, tucking her cigarette behind her ear.

"You're looking good, Tom," she said, voice pitched low enough that Anatoliy wouldn't be able to hear. "Where've you been keeping yourself these past few years?"

"I thought everyone knew?" Sam unloaded his submachine gun, packed it away.

Rayen shook her head, rested her hand on his upper arm, her flat black nail polish seeming to suck up the light compared to his gleaming metal arm. "They didn't think to tell me. Or Anatoliy, I think. You've kept yourself in shape."

"You're hitting on me?"

Something sparkled in her dark eyes. "Could be. Do you mind?"

Tom gently removed her hand from his arm. "Could be I already have someone."

"So? I'm not suggesting anything permanent. Besides," she whispered into his ear, "it could be fun."

Tom shook his head. "I don't think that would be a good idea. I have a girlfriend."

"Really? You? Huh. What's she like?"

"She's a str- errr exotic dancer."

Rayen arched an eyebrow at Tom. "And you're okay with your girlfriend taking her clothes off for strangers?"

Tom shrugged. "It's better than what I do for a living."

"Okay. But still, don't you think the two of us could have some fun? I mean I've always-"

"Sam's coming back over."

Rayen moved so quickly to the other side of the table, Tom had to blink and wonder if the conversation had happened at all.

"Okay, people, are we almost done here?"

"Yeah," Tom said, looking around. They'd cleared the place out. There were still the two vans and Shaman's bike, but everything was loaded up... except for Ju-Won. "What about him?"

Sam frowned, looked at the other members of the team. "What do you mean?"

"We can't leave him here, can we?" Tom asked.

Shaman shook his head. "They'd probably find a way to tie him back to us."

"So what do you suggest?"

"We still have some thermite left," Anatoliy offered.

Tom blinked. "You sure about that?"

Anatoliy nodded. "Yeah, should take care of any implants he has as well."

Tom looked down at Ju-Won, his dead face slack and emotionless.

He remembered Ju-Won for his acerbic personality, his facility with computers and networks, and his perverse drive to turn systems against themselves. None of that was evident now. So what did it matter if they incinerated this lifeless shell? Whatever made Ju-Won Ju-Won had bled out with his life.

"Yeah, okay," he said.

Tom helped Anatoliy lay Ju-Won's body down on the concrete. Shaman applied set up the thermite, but passed the magnesium flare to light it to Sam. "You should have the honors, I think."

Sam frowned, and Tom realized, seeing the hard edges worn into his face, how old he was. He took the flare and stared at it for a moment, as if trying to remember what it was he was supposed to be doing. "It is no honor," he said. He lit the flare, tossed it on top of the thermite covered corpse. "Good-bye Ju-Won."

"All right, let's clear out. Rayen, Anatoliy, you've got the vans. I've contacted the buyers and they've agreed to a hand-off tomorrow. I'm texting you the coordinates now for where we'll meet up. I expect this to all go smooth, but, well, I think we've all been in this business long enough to know that smooth is a pipe dream. Get some rest, and I'll see you all tomorrow."

Tom's eyes narrowed, but he nodded his agreement. He didn't like the idea of splitting up before the meet, but he also realized that the warehouse was going to be too hot.

"Need a lift somewhere?" Rayen asked, the window rolled down, and the lit cigarette hanging from her bottom lip.

Tom shook his head. "I'm good. Need to get my head clear. A walk will help."

She shook her head and smirked. "Suit yourself."

Tom headed out from the warehouse, no real destination in mind. As he walked, he dialed Sunny.

"Tom?" she sounded groggy. He checked the time stamp and realized how late it was.

"Sorry, Sunny. I should have waited until morning."

"No, it's okay. Everything all right? Job go okay?"

"Mostly." He took a deep breath, wished that his filtration mask let him smoke a cigarette. He'd have to wait. His chest ached with a deep pain where he'd been shot. "We lost one of the crew."

"Shit, Tom. I'm sorry. Were you close?"

Tom leaned against a wall, and closed his eyes. He thought back over the missions he had with Ju-Won, the beers they had bonded over. Truth to tell, they had precious little in common other than the job.

"No, I guess not. Always hard to have someone die on you though, isn't it?"

"I dunno. I guess. Look, I know this is hard, but can you call me tomorrow?"

"Yeah, sure, sorry."

"Don't be, Tom. I'm half-asleep at the moment, and now is not the best time, okay? But please, don't feel bad, all right? Call me tomorrow though, okay?"

"Yeah, if I can. Supposed to finish the deal tomorrow."

"Fine, but call me all right? I mean it."

"Yeah, and thanks Sunny."

He heard her yawn on the other end of the line. "G'night, Tom."

"Good night, Sunny."

Tom spent the rest of the night walking back to his apartment, the distant wail of sirens accompanying him as they sped toward a warehouse ablaze.

EIGHT

The phone in his head ringing woke Tom up. He sat up, his gun already in his hand. He shook his head and answered the phone.

"Mr. Costigan?" Tom recognized the voice as belonging to one of the agents from the other night.

"Yeah?"

"We are disappointed, Mr. Costigan." The agent's voice was flat and level. It reminded Tom of combat pilots he'd run into. It didn't matter how much shit was flying at them, they always possessed the same level tone. "One of our holdings was hit last night."

"Sorry to hear that." Tom got out of bed, with a groan, his chest still hurting. He didn't put his gun away. "You don't think I had anything to do with that, do you?" Tom wondered how they got a hold of his number, decided that was the least of his concerns at the moment.

"We are... unsure. Which is why we are currently having this conversation. If we knew-" The speaker let the threat hang in the air, pregnant with possibility.

"Yeah, I get it. So what do you want?"

"Mr. O'Dell has not been in contact with you?"

Tom found his cigarettes, slipped one between his lips. "Nope."

"And you would tell us if he did?"

"Don't know. I do like it better when you call then when you show up unannounced though."

"You returned to your apartment late last night."

Tom chuckled, though he felt the hairs on the back of his neck go up. "Keeping track of me? What you don't trust me?"

"Trust but verify, Mr. Costigan. We'll be in touch."

"Yeah." The phone disconnected.

Tom checked the time. He still had a few hours before we was supposed to go to the rendezvous. He looked in his small microfridge, saw he still had a protein shake. It was about all he could afford on his day wage. He swallowed the thick, congealed liquid down, tried hard not to think about where the protein came from. He wiped his mouth on the back of his sleeve and chucked the empty container into the recycling chute. He sat on the bed, the worn springs protesting, and lit his cigarette. He breathed in, felt the smoke tickle the back of his throat. He sucked it down to the filter, before stubbing it out on the ashtray next to his bed. He got up, got dressed. He looked down at the pistol before finally tucking it into its holster, securing it under his jacket, its bulk hidden under his clothes.

He stepped out of his apartment, front door this time. He waited until he was in his building's lobby before putting on the filtration mask. It was still hours before the rendezvous, but it gave Tom time to walk. Besides, his apartment, with its peeling paint and industrial aesthete seemed designed to breed depression. He was having a hard enough time processing events as it was. Easier to put one foot in front of the other, focus on the simple task of walking.

He found himself in a diner, staring down at an empty coffee cup, trying to remember how he got there. He checked the time. He hadn't missed the rendezvous yet, but it was getting close. He called a cab, gave a destination eight blocks from he was supposed to go. The driver gave him an odd look when Tom paid and got out.

"Sure you don't want me to stick around?" the cabbie asked, eyes barely drifting away from his meter. "This is... not so good a neighborhood."

Tom flashed a smile. "It's all right." He pulled the sleeve back on his jacket, revealing his arm. "I can handle myself."

The cabbie shook his head and muttered something in a language Tom didn't recognize. He understood the sentiment though.

This part of the city was overgrown and falling apart. Most of the houses still standing were boarded up or burnt out, scared and angry eyes peered out from the windows of the ones still occupied. Tom spotted a pack of wild dogs staring at him from a corner. The otherwise constant buzz of drones was quieter out here.

This was the part of the City everyone liked to forget about. Where wage slaves came to die, or where people who didn't quite fit in were pushed out to. It wasn't a bad place to come to score drugs, as long as all you wanted was some pedestrian shit and nothing too exotic. No one bothered Tom as he walked through the neighborhood, because as soon as he'd stepped out of the cab his, whole stance had changed. He walked like he belonged, and in many ways he did. Tom had grown up in a neighborhood like this, so he understood the pain and anger, understood what could make a kid make some bad choices along the way and end up on the wrong side of a prison wall. He hawked and spat, pushing those memories back down.

He found the address Sam had given him. The windows were dark and boarded up. He walked around to the back, saw the vans parked along with Shaman's bike, the lawn long since gone to seed. Rayen sat on the back step, her long legs stretched out in her faux-leather pants, a half-smoked cigarette dangling from her lip.

"Wasn't sure you were going to make it."

Tom checked his internal time. "I'm early."

She smiled at him, a lop-sided grin that betrayed nothing of what she was thinking. "Not by much. Come on in, the others are waiting."

She stood up and opened the door. Despite looking like it was boarded up, that's all it was, a clever deception. Inside, Sam had set up a command post. Along one wall, he had posted aerial footage of a parking garage. Surrounding it were a number of tall buildings. Tom thought it looked to be on the outskirts of the city, close to where the wilderness took over.

"That's the rendezvous?"

Sam looked up from the laptop screen her was bent over. "Yes, and it was mutually agreed on. Why, you don't like it?"

"You don't think it's too exposed?" Tom asked.

Shaman was sitting at a table, recalibrating the scope on his rifle. He put it down, rested his hands behind his head. "The plan is we meet under the concrete."

Tom wrinkled his nose. "Where are you going to be?"

Shaman stood up, walked over to a street map. A number of pins had been stuck into it at various points. "Covering your exit here," he said, tapping one pin.

"Anatoliy will be with us for the hand off. Rayen drives."

Tom scratched the side of his nose. "And me?"

"Helping with the actual hand off. I need someone cool under pressure, Tom. Are you my guy?"

Tom nodded. "Yeah." He studied the maps and photographs again. "You sure we can trust these guys?"

A door opened and Anatoliy emerged from a set of stairs leading down into a basement, a large duffel slung across his back. "We can only trust each other." He reached back and tapped the side of the bag of he was carrying. "For everyone else, we have guns." He placed the bag down on the ground, gentle as a baby. Tom could only guess what kind of munitions Anatoliy was planning on bringing along.

"Speaking of which," Sam said, "I figured you'd want to arm up." He led Tom into what would normally be a living room. Inside was an array of military grade hardware. A few sniper rifles, several assault rifles, even a squad automatic weapon. Tom walked over, ran his hand over one of the carbines. He selected a fairly standard looking assault rifle, a few magazines worth of ammunition. He also made sure to grab a bulletproof vest, considering one had saved his life the last time.

"Expecting bear?" he asked, one eyebrow raised.

Sam shrugged at him and smiled. "Could be we won't find anything. But you know me, Tom. Always an abundance of caution. Besides, it's always good to put on a show, especially when you don't know what to expect from the opposite party."

"Yeah. So this is a cash deal?" Tom asked.

Sam shook his head. "No, cryptocurrency."

Tom frowned. "But we don't have a hacker."

"Ju-Won set us up. I made sure that was taken care of before we went in."

"Always a step ahead of everyone else, Sam."

Sam stared hard at Tom, then hawked and spat on the floor. "I reckon that's why I'm still alive."

"If you boys are quite done," Rayen interjected. "If we're going to make the rendezvous on time we need to leave five minutes ago."

"You heard her, boys," Sam said. "Mount up and let's go. We'll come back here after the meet, you'll get paid, and we'll go our separate ways. Neat and tidy."

Tom got into the back with Anatoliy. Rayen drove the van, with Sam riding shotgun. Shaman took off on his bike in order to set up, his saddlebag concealing his broken down sniper rifle. Anatoliy punched Tom in his shoulder. "Are you okay? You seem a thousand miles away."

Tom shook his head, frowned at the floor of the van. "I don't know. Maybe Ju-Won's death hit me harder than I thought." He blinked his eyes, focused on his hands. "I'll be glad when the job's done."

Anatoliy smiled. "Me too. I have missed working with you, though. You were always... understanding. Never judging. Not like some."

Tom chuckled. "Yeah, well glass houses and all that."

"I do not think I understand."

"I'll explain it to you when this is all said and done over a beer."

Anatoliy cracked a wide smile. "Now that I understand."

Sam twisted around in his seat. "Will you two ladies hush up back there. We're about fifteen minutes from the meet. I suggest you make sure you're ready."

Tom slipped on the vest and made sure it was secure. He checked the action on his rifle, and made sure he could get his pistol and his knife clear if he needed them. Not that he hoped he would need them. He closed his eyes and hoped for a clean swap.

"You think it will go badly?" Anatoliy asked, his voice barely audible over the noise of the engine.

Tom shrugged, wished for a cigarette and realized it was a bad idea in the close confines of the van. "Maybe? I don't know enough about the people we're dealing with. That always makes me nervous."

"But Sam knows them. He trusts them. Isn't that enough?"

"Maybe," Tom replied. But he didn't think that was enough.

They rode the rest of the way in silence, Tom checking his gun, making sure the grenades were sufficiently attached to the combat webbing over his ballistic vest. Rayen pulled into the parking garage. The thought of all that concrete over his head gave Tom some comfort, shielding them from the prying electronic eyes of drones and satellites. It also meant Shaman would be unable to help them if things went to shit.

Two SUVs were waiting for them, men standing around, obviously armed and waiting. Tom recognized the type. Corporate security goons, armed with standard off the shelf pistols and submachineguns, dressed in suits that could stop a low caliber round but wouldn't do much against anything serious. He wondered if any of them were sporting cybernetics, but he reckoned if they were they probably believed hiding them was the tasteful thing to do. They might have done a turn down in LatAm or in one of the brush fire wars down in Africa, but at the end of the day they weren't better than any other wage slave, collecting a steady paycheck. Then again, thinking about his crappy apartment, maybe there was something to collecting a steady wage after all.

"Are you ready?" Sam asked. Tom fit his filter mask over the bottom half of his face and nodded. "Let's go."

Rayen parked the van so that it was broadside to the opposite party. Anatoliy got out first, his harness already on, his machinegun strapped and loaded. "Make them think twice about a double cross," he said, smiling.

Sam exited from the front, and Tom got out the back, carrying the package. He made sure to hold it in his left hand, leaving his right free to draw a weapon if it came down to it. Just because Sam was sure it was going to all go smooth was no guarantee.

"Mr. O'Dell." An older man stepped forward in a suit several pay grades above that of the other goons. "I trust you have the compound and the information we require?"

Sam held up a flat disc. "Info is right here. My compadre there," he flicked his head back to Tom, "has the compound. Here's how I figure it. We walk the compound over first, you transfer the money over, I give you the info. We all walk away with what we want."

The man looked around, squinted. "You seem to be running light, Mr. O'Dell. I trust you didn't run into any complications."

Tom couldn't see Sam's face, but he could see his body tense. "Nothing we couldn't handle." He shrugged. "You contracted me for results, not for billable hours. Be happy with the results."

The man nodded. "The compound?"

Sam waved Tom forward. Tom stepped forward, one foot in front of the other. He tried to watch everything at once, the people in front of him, the ones standing off to the side, the ones near the back. So far, everyone was cool, hands off of guns and triggers, trying to project an aura of professional calm when everyone was everything but. One of the security guards came over, hands up and empty, and took the compound from Tom. Tom slowly walked backwards, still trying to keep everything in perspective.

"All right, and now the money," Sam said.

The suit smiled, reached into his pocket. In his hand was a small data stick. "You'll find an authorization code on here. Cryptocurrency like you requested, in the sum you asked for."

"Mind if we validate?"

"Not at all." He handed the stick to a different guard who walked it over. Tom kept looking around, thinking that something felt off, like the faint smell of something rotten in the air. Looking over, he caught a glimpse of movement in the shattered window of an apartment. He called up the map, overlaid it in his vision. That apartment was supposed to be abandoned, condemned for years. So why did it look like-

"Get down," he shouted, diving for Sam. The security guard with the data stick stared at Tom for a second, before his head exploded like an overripe watermelon.

45

"Sniper!" the suit yelled, reaching for his gun. "You betrayed us."

Tom and Sam ran for the back of the van, taking cover. "We need that data stick," Sam said. "Anatoliy?"

"I am on it." Anatoliy took a knee and aimed toward the apartment. "Tom? A little help?"

Tom hustled over, trying to keep as low a profile as possible. The security guards on the other side were in chaos, and the man in the expensive suit had disappeared into one of the vehicles. The sniper kept up his fire, taking out another two of the guards. Tom located where the sniper was coming from, helped Anatoliy line the shot. The sound of the machinegun echoed off the concrete, drowning out any other noise.

Tom duck walked away, trying to keep the van between himself and any other active shooters as possible.

"What the hell is going on?" Shaman's voice crackled over Tom's earpiece.

"We've got an active situation. Sniper," Sam replied. "Whole thing has turned into a shit show. How soon do you think you can get here?"

"On my way now."

"Anatoliy?"

"Missed the fucker."

"Tom?"

"Yeah?"

"I'll give you cover. Get that data stick."

"I hate you a little right now."

"Don't care. Go."

Tom ran out. He felt something whizz by his head, saw sparks strike on the concrete, then heard the report of the rifle. "He's still out there," he shouted.

He slid on the ground, catching his ankle painfully underneath him, rolled next to the dead security guard.

"He keeps moving," Anatoliy shouted. "Hard to keep track of which window he'll pop out of next."

Tom pried the data stick from the dead man's hand. He saw the other guards spot him, raise their guns. "Anatoliy, a little help!" He wrenched his assault rifle around and fired a quick burst, catching one guard in his leg. The guard dropped to the ground, and Tom shot him through the head.

The big man turned the machinegun on the security guards, bullets chewing through the thin metal of their vehicles.

"Tom, see if you can get the container." Sam's voice sounded strained through Tom's earpiece. He sprinted over, tried to get the engine block of the vehicle between himself and where he thought the sniper might be positioned. He yanked one of the grenades off his webbing and tossed it near the guards. They dove away from it, one of them falling awkwardly and not getting back up.

Tom tried to pull the door open of the car where he saw the suit enter, but the man had the presence of mind to lock the door. Tom shot the window, the bullets leaving a line of weakened glass easily broken by the butt of his gun. He stuck the barrel of the rifle through the window. "Hand over the container," he barked.

The suit, his hands shaking, passed it to Tom, who tucked it under his arm. "Sure hope you know what you are doing, Sam," he muttered through gritted teeth. As he was getting ready to make the return trip back to the van, he heard the squeal of tires and saw Shaman rocketing toward him on his motorcycle, fat tires hugging the concrete. The sniper slowed down, his hand out as he drove by Tom. , Tom latched his metal hand to Shaman, felt a sharp wrenching pain where his metal arm joined his flesh body but the connection held. He heard the motorcycle emit a weird groan as the stabilization system kicked into overdrive to prevent the entire bike from flipping end over end. Shaman grunted and placed both hands on the handlebars, body kept low as he sped out of the garage.

"You are on your own to get out," Shaman said on the group channel. "I've got Tom."

"Go to the second safe house," Sam replied. "We're following now. Anatoliy, let's go."

Tom held on with his knees as Shaman rocketed through the parking garage, headed straight for the exit. Tom looked over Shaman's shoulder, saw two SUV's blocking their exit. "You've got a plan?"

"Hang on," Shaman replied through gritted teeth. Tom grabbed onto the handles and hunched down as Shaman slalomed between the vehicles. Tom felt the leg of his pants brush against the front bumper of one of the cars, heard people yelling at them, and then they were through.

"You're going to have trouble," Tom relayed through his earpiece. "They've got the exit blocked."

Tom heard a maniacal cackle in response and then the sound of metal crashing as Rayen drove the van through the blockade. The tires squealed on the road, and then it was off in the opposite direction.

"How are we doing Tom?" Shaman asked, weaving the bike in and out of traffic, Tom doing his best to keep his seat and not tumbling off the motorcycle. Even if the cycle was designed to stay upright, it didn't mean Tom couldn't fall off and develop a serious case of road rash.

"Rayen got through." Tom twisted to look back. "Uh, we've got a SUV on our ass though."

"You've got a gun right?"

Tom bit the inside of his cheek and didn't comment. He slipped the compound container into one of Shaman's saddlebags, and made sure the data stick was secured in a pocket. He knew it was going to be awkward to fire the assault rifle, so he pulled out his pistol. Behind him, he saw a figure lean out the passenger window, aim a rifle at them.

"Try to give me a straight run," he said, taking aim. The bike swerved, and he was forced to hold on with his left hand. "Hold still, dammit!"

"I didn't want to pancake into the back of a delivery truck," Shaman hissed back. "You want to drive?"

Tom growled and fired three shots off. The first hit the hood, bouncing off and striking the windshield. It didn't even have the good grace to crack. His second hit the asphalt underneath, ricocheting away. The third punched a hole into the gunman, knocking him back. He hung lifeless out of the window before striking the back of another car. That's when he saw two more people lean out with their guns. He saw the muzzle flashes, heard the angry bee whine of the bullets as they sped by. Windows from nearby cars shattered as they were struck by bullets, and sparks shot up where they hit the street near the motorcycle.

"Having trouble?" Shaman asked.

"Yeah, a bit," Tom answered. He pulled a grenade out, tried to time the release. He let it go, but the SUV swerved right, and it exploded, taking out a sedan car.

"No luck?"

"Fuck you."

"Sorry, not my type."

Tom tried for a tire and was sure he'd hit, but the car kept driving with no sign of any damage. "Fuck shit damn piece of shit pistol," he muttered under his breath.

"Can I help you?" Shaman asked, weaving between cars as bullets flew around them. "Not sure how long it's going to be before they get lucky."

"Yeah." Tom holstered the pistol, grabbed onto the motorcycle with his flesh and blood hand, and brought the assault rifle around with his left hand. He sent a mental command and the arm went rigid and unbending, the only part still flexible was his trigger finger. "Can you get next to them? Left side, if you can."

"I hope you know what you're doing," Shaman replied. Tom fired a burst at the passenger side of the SUV, clipping the windshield, and sending the gunmen on that side diving back in. This time he saw cracks appear in the windshield as the higher powered rounds were able to punch through.

Shaman hit the brakes, tires squealing, and Tom could smell the burnt rubber even through his filtration mask. The SUV shot forward, and then they were abreast. Tom pulled the trigger, firing through the SUVs open window. Blood sprayed out, and the SUV swerved out of control as the driver slumped against the wheel. Shaman sped the motorcycle ahead and to the right, narrowly missing a slow-moving municipal bus in the process.

"Nice," Shaman said as Tom let himself relax. "Sam, we're headed to the safe house now."

That's when the drone opened up above them. The bike fell apart in a pinwheel of chrome and steel, sending Shaman flying off away from Tom. Tom managed to get his left arm mostly underneath himself. It still hurt, but his armor saved him from the worst of the road rash. He rolled and came to a stop against a concrete abutment. He pushed himself, slowly, to his feet, every fiber of his being screaming in pain. He limped toward the wreckage of the bike, trying to keep an eye on the sky in case the drone made another pass.

"Shaman?"

Shaman picked up his head, stared at Tom with his one remaining good eye. The left side of his face was a mashed pulp, and his left arm hung at the wrong angle, bending the wrong way in at least three places. Both legs were bent at odd angles, his armored coat shredded where he'd scraped along the ground. He smiled at Tom, then coughed, blood spattering his lips. Tom could see where the skin had been split open, revealing bone and metal both.

"Think I'm done, Tom."

Tom knelt down, cars still screaming by, making it hard to hear if the drone was going to make another pass. "Bullshit, I'll find a car. I'll get us to the safe house."

Shaman shook his head, winced and coughed again. "Not this time. Get the compound though. Don't trust O'Dell."

Tom blinked. "What?"

Shaman used his one working arm to pass over the container with the chemical compound.

"Give me a cigarette?"

Tom fumbled in his jacket pocket, found half of one. He looked apologetic to Shaman.

"No worries. I don't think I could smoke a full one anyway."

Tom lit the cigarette and took a puff before placing it between Shaman's bruised and busted lips. "Think these things will kill me?" Shaman asked with a tortured laugh.

"Why shouldn't I trust Sam?"

Shaman looked at Tom, blinked his one working eye. "Do we know what this compound is, Tom? Do we know who we're working for?"

"Why didn't you say something sooner?"

Shaman smiled, tired and sad and hurt. "Because I wanted the paycheck. Same as everyone else. Doesn't matter now." Shaman's eye rolled up, his smile becoming a frown. "You better go, Tom. Go to ground. Find out what Project Prometheus does. Hell, ditch the container and go to ground. You can probably live like a king off what's on the data stick."

Tom ran his tongue along the inside of his mouth and tasted copper. In the distance he could hear sirens, growing closer.

"Go on, Tom," Shaman said. "They're playing my song."

Tom handed Shaman his last grenade, placing it in his shattered hand. He pulled the pin and helped Shaman close his hand around it.

Tom ran the strap from the container around his shoulder. He ditched the assault rifle next to Shaman, but made sure to keep his pistol, glad that he hadn't lost it when the motorcycle had crashed. He mentally switched off the phone in his head and headed down a side street, trying hard to ignore the pain in his leg and the hard stares he was receiving. Behind him, he heard the muffled whump of the grenade going off.

Overhead, the gray skies darkened and a bitter cold rain began to fall.

NINE

Tom knocked on the steel security door, metal banging against metal. He looked into the unblinking lens of the security camera and gave it the finger.

"Tom? Jesus Christ, what happened?" Sunny opened the door and stepped aside. She'd dyed her hair purple, and recently given how bright it was. Tom limped into her apartment, dropping his bag as he walked. He took the container with the chemical off his shoulder and placed it on the floor. He looked around, weary.

"Something go wrong with the job?" Sunny asked, helping Tom get his jacket off.

Tom chuckled, a dry, raspy sound that sounded worse than he intended. "Yeah. You still got those extra clothes I stashed here?"

"Yeah, give me a second, will you?"

"Got nowhere else to be."

She disappeared into her back room. Tom knew she stored most of her stuff back there, old computer parts for the most part which she swore she'd need one day. The main living space was dominated by her rig. Thirteen monitors, an oversized keyboard, a couple of webcams, and half a dozen servers strung together in a seeming haphazard pattern. Everything was in standby mode, so the room was bathed in a soft blue glow, all the other lights having been turned off.

As he waited, he stripped off his jacket and shirt, wincing as the cloth stuck to abraded skin. He looked for a place to put the bloody fabric, and finally settled for the floor.

"Hey, Sunny who was that... oh." A woman stood in the door, her silver circuitry tattoos standing in contrast to her dark skin. Her head was shaved, and Tom saw light glint off the metal studs by her ears. "Uh, hi."

Tom nodded back. "Uh, hey. Sorry about this. I'm Sunny's..."

Sunny came back into the room at that point. "Hey, Tom, I found this duffel bag that I think is yours. No way I was going to go digging around in it. I don't need to touch your boxers." She stopped, looked from the woman to Tom and back to the woman. "Well , this is awkward."

The woman leaned against the doorframe, arms crossed. "Are you going to introduce me to your boyfriend?"

Both Tom and Sunny laughed, which Tom immediately regretted as it hurt like hell. "I'm her brother," he said, wheezing and holding his side. "Name's Tom."

The woman blinked, looked over at Sunny who looked down at her feet. "Brother?"

Tom chuckled which turned into a groan. "Can I sit down? Maybe on something you won't mind if I bleed on a little?"

"Get over here," Sunny said. In addition to the duffel bag, she also had her black medical bag.

"Go start a pot of water to boil, Cheyenne."

Cheyenne shook her head and walked into the narrow galley of a kitchen.

"Trouble in paradise?" Tom asked.

"Sit. Down." Sunny directed Tom to sit down on a sofa, but not before putting down some clear plastic sheeting. "Don't need you bleeding on everything."

"You're all heart."

Sunny opened her medical bag, started looking through her options. "Want something for the pain?"

Tom shook his head. "Job's not done yet," he said.

Sunny narrowed her eyes at him. "So why are you here? What happened?"

Tom dropped his voice to a whisper. He could hear Cheyenne banging around in the kitchen, making enough noise so that they knew she wasn't actively eavesdropping. "There was an ambush at the meet. We got away, but then a drone hit us. Me and Shaman anyway. I don't know about the other three."

"Where's Shaman?"

Tom shook his head, regretted it as pain shot through his back and neck. "I took the hit better than he did."

"Oh. So is this what you were after?" Sunny kicked the container.

"Yeah. Something called Prometheus. Whatever that means?"

Cheyenne stuck her head out from the kitchen. "Prometheus was the Titan that stole fire from the Gods on Olympus and gave it to humanity. Kind of a big deal in Greek mythology."

Tom smiled. "So a Robin Hood kinda guy. I can get behind that." He sucked in a hard breath as Sunny applied antiseptic to his wounds, layered a gauze bandage over it. "Guess he got away with it to, seeing as how we have fire and all."

Cheyenne shook her head. She walked over, craning her neck to see what Sunny was doing. "You really are shit at this aren't you? Shove over."

Sunny moved, sticking her bottom lip out at her girlfriend. "I've been patching up Tom longer than I've been writing code."

"Yeah? Than I thought you'd be better at it. How are your legs?"

"No idea," Tom said. "I walked here though, so they can't be that bad."

"Uh-huh. Lose the pants, or what's left of them."

"Uhm."

"What, don't want to strip down in front of your sister's girlfriend? Trust me, I've seen it all, and you can leave the boxers on."

Tom shucked off his boots and the pants, grimacing as it pulled at the recent wounds.

"Rethinking that painkiller?" Cheyenne asked.

"No, can't afford to get cloudy."

"Uh-huh." Cheyenne went to work with a needle and thread, stitching a flap of skin that had torn loose. "Get into a lot of crashes?"

"More than I like. Why?"

"You might want to invest in a good set of leathers. They won't do you much good in a serious crash, but they'll keep you looking pretty for the funeral."

"Thanks, I'll keep that in mind. You didn't tell me what happened to Prometheus."

"The Gods chained him to a rock, so a giant bird could come by and eat his liver. Only Prometheus was immortal, so the liver regrew every night and every morning that big damn bird came by and got to have breakfast. Every single morning."

Tom eyed the container. "Huh. So what you're saying is I should ditch it."

Cheyenne shrugged. "Your call. Personally I'd find a big black hole to throw it down." She smiled at Tom, a sly, sideways thing that made her look older than he first thought. "But that's just me. You probably want to get paid."

"Can you hand me my pants?"

Cheyenne raised an eyebrow at Tom, but did as he asked.

"Thank you." He fished around in one of the pockets and produced the data stick. "Hey, Sunny."

"Yeah?" She looked up from her computer rig. "What've you got Tom?"

"My payday. Maybe. The deal was for cryptocurrency. I think it might be on here."

Sunny wrinkled her nose. "So you got the whole kit? Chemical and pay both? Why Tom, we might make a real criminal out of you yet."

Tom shook his head. "Sam still had the data, I think the how of making the stuff, whatever it is. Hell, he probably has exactly what it does from the data we stole."

Cheyenne pulled back, looked Tom over. "You can get dressed now."

"Thanks."

"So does Sam know where you are?" Sunny asked.

"I doubt it. I never talked about you, and turned the phone off as soon I left Shaman."

"Huh? What phone?" Cheyenne asked.

Tom tapped the side of his head. "I kept misplacing mine, so got one of those shots. You know the one, turns your jaw into transmitter. I make sure to download the latest patches from my very own security expert." He smiled at Sunny as he pulled on the pants from the duffel bag.

Cheyenne blinked at him. "Oh. So how much of you is human?"

Tom frowned slightly. "More than fifty percent. Easily. All the internal stuff," he tapped his chest, "is original. The arm... well, not that so much, but it's probably the reason I'm still alive. I managed to land on it when we crashed and it absorbed most of the damage."

"Yeah, I meant to ask you about that," Sunny said. "Any trouble with it?"

Tom moved his arm around, making sure he could lift, lower and twist it. He opened and close his fist. "No trouble."

"All right, let's take a look at the data stick then." Sunny took it from Tom, slotted it into one of the myriad ports on her rig. "Well this isn't good."

"Huh? What's wrong?" Tom asked.

"Take a look."

Tom limped over to Sunny, wondering if he should have maybe taken that painkiller he'd been offered. He squinted at the screen. "What am I looking at here?"

"You said this was supposed to be in cryptocurrency right? He ever say what kind?"

Tom shook his head. "No idea. Why?"

Sunny sighed. "Here's the thing. Yeah, there's probably a way to access the funds."

"But?"

"It's asking for a very specific password. I'm guessing they've used machine derived encryption. And we don't have the key."

Tom wrinkled his nose. "But why would they give Sam a data stick and not the key?"

"Who arranged the deal with the buyers?" Sunny asked.

Tom frowned, his brow furrowing into deep lines. "Sam did."

Sunny nodded. "Yeah, and if he was smart, what he did was provided the buyer with the encryption key as part of the original negotiation. They would have encrypted the data stick, this way if it fell into the hands of a third party they wouldn't be able to access the data. Pretty savvy if you ask me."

"Anyway you can crack it?"

Sunny raised her eyebrow at Tom. "You got a couple of hundred years?"

Tom blinked at her. "No."

"Yeaah, didn't think so." Sunny typed at her keyboard, her fingers a blur. On the screen lines of code appeared and scrolled fast enough that Tom couldn't be quite sure what she was looking at.

"Oh, yay. Whoever did this also built into it that it will delete the data after three failed attempts. They also have it protected against copying to a different medium, so I can't just copy the key over and try it from a different device."

Tom blinked at her. "In English?"

"She's saying you need the key," Cheyenne said.

Tom sighed. He walked aback over to the duffel bag, slipped the t-shirt over his head, wincing as it brushed over his recent bandages. "Okay. Looks like I need to call Sam then, figure out our next move."

"You think that's a good idea?" Sunny asked.

"Not even a little bit," Tom replied. "Given that I don't even know what it was we stole though I'm not seeing a lot of other choices."

"You could always walk away," Sunny suggested. "You're not though, are you?"

"No, I don't think I can on this one. Thanks for patching me up, Cheyenne. Sorry for crashing your party."

Cheyenne chuckled. "Yeah, well, Sunny was going to have to tell me about her big badass brother sooner or later. I guess there are worse ways to find out."

Tom smirked. "Yeah, well, I would have preferred a way that involved me bleeding less." He sat down and pulled on his boots. "I'm going to take a walk before I give Sam a call. We lost our hacker, but, well, I'm not sure how much I trust him right now."

Sunny came over, leaned down and gave him an awkward huh. "Keep me posted, all right?"

Tom patted her back with his right arm. "Yeah, I'll do that. And Sunny?"

"Yeah?"

"Thanks."

TEN

"Tom?"

"Yeah, Sam."

"What the hell happened? You went completely dark and didn't show up at the rendezvous. What happened?"

"We got hit with a drone strike on our way to meet you. I went to ground for a while." Tom leaned against a concrete wall, gang tags etched into the wall with acid-based paint. Harder to pressure wash off that way. He reached into his pocket for his cigarettes, then remembered he had given his last one to Shaman.

"Do you still have the package? The data stick?" There was a manic edge to Sam's voice.

"Aren't you going to ask me about Shaman?"

"I figured he was still with you."

"Shaman's dead, Sam."

"Fuck."

"Yeah, well, funny how you didn't ask me about him first." Tom watched as a four man riot patrol walked by. They side-eyed Tom but didn't give him any hassle. That told him whoever was after Prometheus didn't want to get the authorities involved. He figured he looked like he belonged enough for them not to give him too much hassle. He made sure to keep the prosthetic out of sight, just to be sure.

"Trying to say something, Tom?"

"No. I'm not looking for a fight. I'm tired is all. Been a long day." Tom pinched the bridge of his nose. "You still at the rendezvous?"

"No, we moved on. After you went dark, we had no way of knowing if you and Shaman had gotten picked up. No offense, Tom, but anyone can break under pressure."

"Yeah. Want to send me coordinates to come to you?"

"Sending them now. Be sure you aren't followed, all right?"

"Yeah, all right. Not my first rodeo, Sam."

Sam chuckled. "Yeah, but if we play this right, it could be the last one you need." The line clicked off. A message popped up in his heads-up display with the GPS coordinates for the new safe house. Tom wondered just how many bolt holes Sam had around the city.

"You get all that, Sunny?" Tom asked.

"I got it. Running the trace on his location now."

"Here's the coordinates he gave me. Do they match?"

"No. The trace is about six kilometers off from that. He could be bouncing the signal in case anyone is trying to trace it back though. Hard to tell, and you weren't talking for long enough for me to check."

Tom sighed. "Okay, so any idea what I'm walking into?"

Sunny sighed. "It's a track of apartment buildings. Low rent for the most part. Some condemned buildings. Lot of squatters. It would be a good place to lay low. Not a lot of people would be asking questions and the police don't go there unless it's to quell a riot."

"I hear a pretty big 'but' coming."

"Are you making fun of my butt?"

"Sunny."

"Sorry, sorry. Yeah. If I was looking to stage an ambush, there are definitely worse places to do it. High crime area, a few competing gangs. Sam could probably pick up some muscle on the cheap if he needed to."

"Yeah, well, he's got Anatoliy." Tom started walking, hands in pockets, toward the coordinates Sam had given him. He figured it was going to take him a while to get there on his feet, but it would give him time to figure something out.

"I think you mentioned him. Big guy, right? Russian?"

"Ukranian. Likes machine guns to an unhealthy degree. If he's in with Sam this is going to be tough."

"Anyone else?"

Tom sucked on his teeth. "Rayen. Driver and pilot. I'm... not sure about her."

"Is that 'cause you slept with her?"

"I didn't sleep with her, and even if I did I don't see how that's any of your business."

"Ah, because you want to sleep with her. Or she offered at least."

"Sunny," Tom said, his voice carrying a measure of heat with it.

"Yeah, yeah, none of my business. Careful Tom, you always get twisted when it comes to women. I mean, just look at you and Shari."

"Now is really not the time, Sunny."

"So what are you going to do then?"

Tom tapped his fist against the ballistic vest under his coat. He cracked a smile, even though he knew Sunny couldn't see it. "Go see, Sam. See if we can strike a deal, renegotiate my contract. I figure you've got Prometheus and the data stick, so if he kills me you can keep it from him."

"Yeah, I'd really prefer a scenario where you don't end up dead. Mom would kill me if she found out you died and I was involved in any way."

"Me too, Sunny, me too." As Tom walked, he passed a newer looking car. Looked like one of those newer electric cars flooding the market. He realized how tired his feet were. "Care to walk your big brother through grand theft auto?"

Sunny chuckled on the other end. "What are you, twelve still? When are you going to figure this shit out on your own?"

"Why should I when I have you?"

"Yeah, yeah, yeah. Come on, I'll talk you through it."

ELEVEN

Tom parked the car near the GPS coordinates, in between two burned out husks. As he exited the car, he pulled his pistol, keeping his finger off the trigger and the barrel pointed down at the ground. He made sure to keep it down by his leg, hoping to hide its profile. He moved into the shadow of the buildings, squat prefabricated structures designed to be equal parts utilitarian and ugly.

He dialed Sam.

"Hi Tom, you here? I don't see you yet."

"Why was the data stick encrypted, Sam?"

Sam chuckled. "Since when did you become a tech head?"

"Since you were getting paid in cryptocurrency," Tom countered.

"What, don't you trust me?" Sam asked. "Come on Tom, don't tell me you went to an outside source."

Tom laughed. "We hadn't worked together in five years, Sam. Got to believe I've resources you don't know about."

Sam sighed. "All right. But I've got the data still, and the buyer. You've got a container of useless goop and a data stick you can't access. What play are you trying to make here, Tom? I've been straight with you, so what do you have to worry about?"

"What about the sniper, Sam? You're going to tell me you didn't know about him?" Tom tried a door, found it opened with a bit of pressure from the cybernetic arm.

"What are you getting at, Tom?"

"He targeted the other side first, and not the big guy with the machine gun and not me. It's like he was abetting a double cross."

"I think you are giving me too much credit, Tom. Come on in out of the cold. We'll get paid. You don't trust me after that, fine. No skin off my back. I'm hoping to retire on this anyway, remember?"

"Yeah, that's what you keep saying. So what does Prometheus do again?"

"No idea." Sam started sounding exasperated. "What do you care?"

"Maybe I gained a conscience sometime in the last five years. Maybe I'm curious. Maybe I just want to make sure if you shoot at me while I'm carrying it that it doesn't eat through my clothes if you rupture the container." Tom found a stairwell and climbed the stairs, carefully putting his foot on each one and pushing up to reduce the noise. He got to the third floor and entered a hallway. He adjusted his eyes for the dim light, the hallway lights long burned out. He crept along, black blooms of mildew on the walls, the floor distressingly spongy beneath his boots.

"Now why would I kill you, Tom?"

"That's what I keep asking myself."

Tom came to a door, already half-opened. He heard voices from within. "Yeah, so when the guy enters the courtyard, we're to pop him, okay? He goes down and then we get paid."

Tom backed up a bit. "Sam, I'm going to have to call you back."

"Tom, wait-" but Tom had already silenced his phone.

He drew a breath, then went right at the door, crashing into it shoulder first. Inside were three men, scabbed arms and ratty hair, patchwork clothes and jittery movements. They froze, unsure of what to do, their brains frozen in indecision. Even suppressed, the pistol was loud in the enclosed space. He drilled two of the gangers, catching them center of mass. The third reached for his gun, but Tom was on top of him, his metal arm grabbing him by his flesh and blood appendage. The ganger screamed and Tom popped him in the mouth with the butt of his pistol.

"Shh." Tom said, pressing the barrel of the gun against the ganger's head. "Where's Sam?"

"Man, fuck you, I don't know who the fuck you're talking about."

Tom rolled his eyes and popped the ganger in the cheek with his pistol. "Guy who paid you to pop me." He held up the cyberarm for the ganger to see. He saw the ganger's eyes go wide in recognition. "Yeah, see. That look. I know that look. It's the look that says 'I'm fucked' and I have no idea how to get unfucked. Here's a hint. Where's Sam?"

The ganger shook his head. "Man, I don't know. He said he'd find us when the job was done. Had this big guy with him, swear he looked like two people put together. Told us it would be easy money."

Tom shook his head. "Ain't no such thing." He smashed the butt of the pistol against the ganger's temple, dropping him to the ground.

He called Sam. "Your boys missed," he said.

"Tom." Sam's voice was flat and angry.

"You had to know I was going to survey the area. You didn't think I'd walk into a killing zone did you? How many other gangs did you pay to hunt me down?"

"Where are you Tom? We can talk this out face to face."

"What's the key to the encryption, Sam? I'll trade Prometheus to you for that."

"That's not the deal on the table, Tom."

"Let me guess, I give you Prometheus and the data stick and what? You'll forget the whole thing? I'll get to walk away and be thankful for it?"

Sam sighed. "Why didn't you come to the safe house, Tom? Yeah, Shaman got killed, but I know you Tom. You could have made it there on your own. Why'd it take you so long to make contact? Who else were you talking to? Making a deal with someone else?"

"It's not like that, Sam. I went to ground because I was hurt and needed patching up." Tom paused, ears straining. He thought he heard the heavy tread of a boot on the floor outside. He placed his finger on the trigger. "Problem is, that also gave me time to think, ask some questions I hadn't thought of before."

The footsteps stopped outside the apartment. Tom moved into what had been the kitchen. All the appliances had been stripped out, nothing left but their outlines against the walls. He pressed against the wall, heard muffled voices from the hallway. Muting his phone, he raised the pistol, put four bullets through the wall, chest high. The rounds punched through the thin interior walls, and the talking turned into screaming. Tom went low as the people outside returned fire, their guns sounding like thunder compared to the dull whump of his own gun. He kept moving, staying low. A figure entered the apartment, a shotgun held low by his hip. It walked past Tom, and he grabbed the barrel with his cybernetic hand and put a bullet where its head was. Another figure came in the room, lighting up the room as he pulled the trigger, a wordless battle cry filling the room as he fired. Tom stepped in close, knocking the gun aside as he moved. The bullets hit the ganger Tom had just killed, his body only know falling to the ground. Tom whipped the shotgun barrel around, clocking the ganger in the side of the head with it, then putting two bullets into him, head and chest.

He flipped his phone off mute.

"You really ought to look into hiring a better class of muscle, Sam."

Tom exited the apartment and headed down the hallway. He checked the bullets for his pistol before holstering it. The shotgun was a pump action with five in the tube.

"I was hoping we could talk this out, Tom," Sam replied.

"I think that ship has sailed." Tom paused at a hallway, quickly poked his head around the corner. Deciding it was all clear, he turned down it. "I tried talking. You set an ambush. You're going to have to do better than that."

"I'm sorry?"

Tom chuckled. "You're apologizing, Sam? Not really a great look for you."

"Figure I could try anything once. What gave it away? Not sincere enough?"

Tom paused, ears straining. He could hear more voices outside, more footsteps echoing through the projects. "Your people are still looking for me, and somehow I don't think they're bringing a card and flowers," Tom replied.

"Well, you know me. Wish for something in one hand and do something with the other."

"Yeah, I know. I learned from you. Which is why I didn't bring the data stick or Prometheus with me."

"Wait, what?"

"Come on, Sam. I had to figure you'd try something like this."

"Well, you started shooting first," Sam countered.

"Seriously?"

"Yeah, I know, a weak argument coming from me."

Tom rounded another corner, a long burned out exit sign signaling a stair well. He opened the door slowly, listened for a moment. Content that there wasn't anyone coming up, he headed down.

"Still, I'd like to know why you're double crossing me. It's not like you know what Prometheus can do, and you sure as shit don't have a buyer for it. Knowing you, you stashed it in a bus stop locker and gave the key to that stripper girlfriend of yours. What's her name, Charlene?"

"Shari, and ex-girlfriend, and ha-ha, no."

"So why did you come here if it wasn't in good faith?"

Tom hit the exit and stayed low by the building. He circled slowly, glad that most of the street lights had long been smashed. He could hear the roving packs of searchers calling to each other. He wondered where Sam was, if he was even in the area or if he was holed up somewhere five miles away, sipping a beer and plotting how best to track Tom down.

"I needed to know for sure you were going to turn on me," Tom said.

"Fuck you, Tom. If you could have opened the data stick without the encryption key you would have disappeared. Six months from now you'd be sipping Mai Thais on a beach while some pretty young thing in a dental floss bikini rubbed sun tan lotion on you."

"You're projecting, Sam. That's your dream."

"Yeah, what's your dream then?"

Tom smiled. He kept to the shadows and made his way away from the apartment complex. "Now that would be telling, Sam. Maybe next time."

"You know you're never going to find a buyer for Prometheus, right? Especially without the information I have. And that data stick is useless without the encryption key."

"Yeah, I get that. But then you need the compound and the data stick. You could've dealt me fair, Sam. Don't put this on me." Tom paused as he watched an overly large shadow detach itself from a wall and head into one of the buildings. So Anatoliy was still alive, and evidently working with Sam. That meant Rayen probably was as well.

"So what's your next move, Tom?"

Tom laughed. "That would be telling." He sidled next to the car he'd stolen and got in, hanging up on Sam. He turned it over, glad for the whisper quiet engine. He kept the lights out until he was out of the area.

"Sunny."

She stifled a yawn on the other end, but it was still loud enough to tell Tom how tired she was. "Everything go okay?"

"If by okay you mean Sam had a bunch of hired guns hanging around waiting for me to show my face, then yeah, it went great."

"Ouch. Everything all right?"

"Yeah, except I'm right back where I started."

"You headed back to your place?"

"No. It's too well known and I don't want to risk going to your place right now. Going to find a rent-a-room and crash for a couple of hours, see if I can get my head straight. Think you can put a call out to any chemists might be willing to pick up a few extra credits?"

"Yeah, maybe. There's a couple of places I can post some vague info, see who bites."

"Okay, do that. I'll drop you a line when I wake up. And Sunny?"

"Yeah, Tom?"

"Thanks."

TWELVE

Tom woke with a start, his hand closing around his pistol. The small room, ten foot on a side, with nothing but a bed, a table, and a hotplate, was otherwise empty. He yawned, stretched, and put on his boots. He checked his internal clock and saw he'd slept for about six hours. He rubbed the sand out of his eyes, dialed Sunny.

"I haven't heard anything yet." She sounded tired, her voice still thick with sleep.

"Nothing at all?"

"Well, nothing worthwhile. More than a few kooks coming out of the woodwork claiming corporate conspiracies and government mind control, but nothing that is actually useful."

Tom scratched the side of his nose. He was craving a cigarette, the internal itch for it crawling up his spine. "Yeah, that's not helpful."

"You think of anything else?"

Tom brought up the phone number he'd been given by the agents in his apartment. "Yeah, not sure I like it though. I could call up the folk who thought it was a good idea to break into my apartment."

"Yeah, I've got to say that isn't what I'd recommend. Anything else?"

"I can go looking for Sam and company. See if I can't steal the key. And the data information. Not sure I like that option much either though."

"Because you don't know where Sam is and you're outnumbered?"

"Yes, that, exactly. Anyway, I'm going to go for a walk. I still have a bit of money. I'm going to see if I can grab something to eat and a pack of smokes."

"You could always take the filtration mask off and take a couple of deep breaths," Sunny suggested.

"Ha. Ha. Very funny. I don't actually want my lungs to collapse."

"So don't smoke."

"Don't take my vices away from me."

"Thought that's what the killing was." Tom could almost hear Sunny's smile.

"That's not a vice, that's business."

"We need to find you another line of work."

"I tried that, remember?" Tom placed his filter mask over his mouth and nose, checked his belongings one more time. He'd had to ditch the shotgun the night before as he didn't have a bag big enough to conceal it, and no tools on hand to cut it down to something more manageable.

Sunny sighed. "Yes, because washing dishes is the only thing you are qualified for." Tom could almost hear her rolling her eyes.

"Going to head out for a while. I'll be in touch, okay?"

"Okay. Be safe."

"Always." Tom hung up the phone and, after giving his room one final look over, opened the door to the hotel. Standing there, pistols raised at Tom's head, were the two agents from his apartment.

"Uh. Hi?" Tom said. He had a thought, a flash like a burning meteorite, of going for his gun. Like a meteorite, that thought was nothing but ash after flaring bright for a moment.

"Mr. Costigan, a word." The two agents pushed him back into the room, and closed the door behind them. Tom noted that neither of them were wearing filter masks, which gave him pause. Either they didn't care about inhaling the toxic sludge atmosphere or their lungs were fundamentally different from what Tom was familiar with.

"Gentlemen, I was about to call you."

The two agents traded a look from behind their sunglasses, their faces remaining expressionless.

"You know where Prometheus is?"

Tom shook his head. "No, not at the moment, but I can confirm that Sam O'Dell has it."

"Yes, we know," the agent on the right said. He was slightly taller than his companion, and his blonde hair was so pale as to be nearly white.

"You know?" Tom's fingers itched for his gun.

The other agent, shorter, his brown hair buzzed into a military cut stared straight at Tom. "We've been monitoring the situation since the break in."

"Ah. So, you know I was in on the job then."

Both men nodded.

Tom blew out a long breath. "How am I still breathing then?"

"Ultimately, you are of no consequence, Mr. Costigan," Blondie said. "We just want Prometheus, and the data, returned to us. We see no reason for further bloodshed."

"You were the ones behind the drone strike. Besides, weren't you the ones telling me that you were going after Sam with, what was it, 'extreme prejudice?' Yeah, no, sorry but I don't think that's the whole story."

Buzzcut pushed Tom back on to the bed. Tom grunted as he fell back, surprised by the strength he felt in that arm. "Been working out?" he asked.

"Why did you take the job, Mr. Costigan? You could have called us, told us that O'Dell had reached out to you. We would have picked him up, written you a nice sized check. We only wanted the ringleader. Your other comrades might still be alive."

"And if wishes were horses," Tom mumbled under his breath. This entire time they did not take their eyes off of him, and their guns didn't waver. "So where do we go from here?"

Buzzcut looked around the apartment. Blondie didn't take his glasses off Tom. "You haven't answered the question, Mr. Costigan. Why did you take the job?"

Tom looked around the small hotel room. "You mean other than the chance to hang out in classy places like this? Well, I was told it was going to pay better than my day job. Can't really say that I'm impressed so far. I can't even get an expense check."

"And if we were to offer you steady employment?"

Tom blinked, placed his hands behind his head. "As what? Sorry, but I draw the line at rough trade."

"As a retrieval expert." The agent said a number. Tom blinked at the number of zeros that would accompany such a figure.

"Just for the container?" Tom asked.

"And the data. One is useless without the other."

"You know this means having to turn against my former comrades. Isn't there like an extra thirty pieces of silver in it for me if I do that?"

Both agents sniffed simultaneously. "Your comrades turned on you first, Mr. Costigan. We had nothing to do with the sniper at the hand-off."

"Yeah, I figured that out already. Okay, okay, get out. I'll see about getting you what you want."

"Do not disappoint us, Mr. Costigan."

"You could use my first name, you know. You keep saying 'Mr.

Costigan' like that, I might think my asshole father is back from the dead."

The two agents turned and walked out of the hotel room. Tom briefly entertained the thought of drilling them in the back of the head with a pair of bullets, but if they were able to breathe the smog of the city unaided then he hesitated to guess what else they might be capable of. Tom raised his hand, formed a gun from his fingers, and mocked shooting at them.

"Right, that was pointless. Time to get to work."

Tom sat at the diner, his coffee no more than a dark ring at the bottom his cup, what was left of the runny eggs smeared across the plate by the toast. He drummed his fingers on the table, then used his headgear to connect to the web. He did a quick search on Kanedex. His eyes narrowed. There wasn't much in the public about them, which didn't surprise Tom. Their public page said they were into cybernetic development and artificial intelligence. He blinked at that, read it again. He went a little deeper into their record, but didn't see much of anything on chemical research and development. He closed that and brought up the local news reports. There wasn't much there, but he did see a few lines about the motorcycle crash and the shootout at the projects. Local police were blaming gang activity, though the reporter did note that high caliber bullets of the kind typically fired from military grade weapons were recovered. Granted, that didn't mean much these days. Lots of folk had access to military grade weaponry, and more than a few veterans from the LatAm or Middle East wars had the tech savvy to create their own.

Tom ran his metal finger through a spot of spilled coffee on the table. He knew he could walk away at this point. Drop Prometheus into a dumpster, and it probably wouldn't be seen again. Leaving the money would hurt, but maybe not as much as going after it would.

His phone rang.

"Hey, Sunny."

Her face came over the live feed, a deep frown etched on her face. "You told me it was a chemical."

Tom raised an eyebrow. "Yeah… because that's what I told it was. It's not? Wait. You opened the container?"

"Yes, I opened the container. I had a few nibbles from people who were interested in looking at the chemical, but they wanted more information on what it might be before they committed. The only way to do that was to open it up."

"What if it was explosive? Or flammable? What if it set the air on fire?""

Sunny snorted. "You should have thought of that before leaving it in my apartment."

"Yeah, I'll give you that. Sorry." Tom signaled to the waitress to refill his cup. "So, not a chemical then?"

"No. Well. Maybe. I mean everything is made up of chemicals, right? So when you get right down to it, that coffee you're drinking is chemicals. Doesn't mean that it's bad, right?" Sunny's voice climbed in pitch, her words coming rapid fire now.

"Sunny."

"Right, sorry Tom." She picked up the camera she was broadcasting with and carried it over to the now open container. Inside a crystal dome, was a twisting, writhing ribbon. It looked like mercury, but it flowed and twisted on its own, snapping back at its own tail. It reflected the available light in scintillating colors, before collapsing into a globe before shooting out tendrils to the surface with an audible thump.

"What. The. Fuck."

"I know right," Sunny swiveled the camera back to her. "I don't what that stuff is, but it seems pretty bleeding edge. As in people will happily make you bleed so they can get their hands on it."

"Yeah, no kidding. And we probably don't want anyone actually getting a closer look at it. Anyway someone could tie your feelers back to you?"

Sunny shrugged and rubbed her nose. "Sure. That's always a risk, right? I was pretty careful though when I reached out. Didn't even use my standard pseudonym. I think I'll be all right."

"Has Cheyenne seen it?" Tom sipped blew over the rim of his coffee cup, took a sip.

"No. I waited until she left for her job. Working at a clinic, can you believe that? She's like the exact opposite of you."

Tom raised an eyebrow. "I'm not going to cause trouble between you two am I?"

Sunny grinned. "I give her a chance to feel sullied. That and I'm really good at-"

"I do not want to know. Okay, so not a chemical per se, or anything like it. Can I say I really want to walk away at this point?"

"Sure, you can say it as much as you want, but I don't think it's going to change anything."

Tom sighed. "Yeah, I get that. I'm halfway tempted to call Kanedex and see if I can give it back to them."

"That's… not a terrible idea," Sunny said. "Do you want me to set it up for you?"

"I wasn't being all that serious, Sunny. Besides, I'm pretty sure Kanedex already has my number. I had another visit from their men-in-black today."

"How'd they track you down?"

"No idea. Maybe they've hacked the local CCTV and ran it through a facial recognition algorithm. Maybe they put a microtracer on me. Or they snuck into my apartment and injected me with something. It doesn't really matter. The short answer is I really can't come by your place any time soon. No reason to give them more leverage than they already have."

"I can take care of myself."

"No. Hell, I can't even help myself in this situation. I can think of a few things I can do though."

"Yeah? How many of them will get you shot?"

"At least three of them." Tom finished his coffee, fished a cred stick out of his pocket to pay. He tensed when he felt a large figure sit down on his right, place a hand the size of a ham on his shoulder.

"Well, as long as we're clear on that."

"Yeah, I'll talk to you later." Tom hung up, turned to look up at Anatoliy who looked at him with a broad grin revealing his large, crooked teeth.

"You are a hard man to find," Anatoliy said, squeezing Tom's shoulder hard enough to make him wince. "I am sorry we missed each other last night."

"Can't say that I feel the same," Tom countered. "Though I've got to wonder how you found me as easily as you did. It's not like this is a small city."

Anatoliy shrugged. "Sam didn't say how he found you. He just woke me up this morning, said 'Anatoliy, go here. You will find our friend, Tom. Bring him here for a chat.' So, here I am." He looked down at Tom's plate and wrinkled his nose. "It should not have come to this."

Tom tried to shrug, but found it impossible with Anatoliy's hand on his shoulder. "Can you blame a man for being nervous?"

Anatoliy snorted. "You ran after the hand off. We could all be rich already. But instead, you panicked and this is where we are now."

"And where is that?" Tom asked.

Anatoliy squeezed Tom's shoulder hard enough he thought he heard a bone creak under the stress. "Come, there is a van waiting for you."

Tom ran his tongue slow over his teeth, tasted the bile rising up in his throat. He thought about going for his gun, but knew that wouldn't do much other than get him killed. "Don't want a cup of coffee first?"

Anatoliy shook his head. "Don't want to keep Sam waiting."

"Yeah, that would be terrible."

Tom got up, Anatoliy's hand still firm on his shoulder, and walked outside, slipping his filtration mask up over his mouth and nose as he passed through the screens of the restaurant. Outside, a black van waited, the window's tinted so he couldn't see who the driver was.

"Get in the back," Anatoliy instructed. Tom went to step up, but Anatoliy stopped him. The big man patted him down, took the gun and the knife both. "Now get in."

Tom smiled. "What, not taking me out to dinner first?" He noted a few passer-bys, all of them studiously ignoring the scene playing in front of him. Inside the van, three gangers stared hard at him.

"There a problem?" Anatoliy asked, shoving Tom in and into a seat. He took a seat directly opposite, hunched over in the tight confines of the van, his massive hands resting on his knees.

"Nope," Tom said, looking at the three gangers. "I don't recognize the new help. Sam's outsourcing now?"

Anatoliy chuckled. "You shouldn't be so surprised, Tom. You met some of their friends last night."

"Ah. That must be why they are looking at me like that then."

"Don't worry, they have strict instructions that they are not to lay hands on you until Sam gives the okay."

"Huh. Somehow that fails to reassure me."

Anatoliy tapped the earpiece he wore. "Okay, Rayen, get us out of here." Tom felt the van accelerate smoothly. He could tell she was working hard not to attract attention.

Tom looked down at this hands. "Not going to bother cuffing me?"

Anatoliy shrugged. "What would be the point?" he asked, tapping Tom on his left shoulder. "Besides, you aren't quite so stupid as to try to escape now." Anatoliy smiled. "No, I think you will wait until we reach our destination and then you will make a break for it." The smile grew wider. "And I will be waiting for you to try."

Tom rolled his neck on his shoulders. "Did you know that we weren't stealing a chemical?"

Anatoliy's smile disappeared and he raised an eyebrow. "What do you know, Tom?"

Tom shrugged. "I opened the container. It wasn't like anything I've ever seen before. Like it was alive somehow."

"Maybe you shouldn't have opened the container, Tom. Maybe you could save everyone a lot of pain if you told me where it was before we see Sam."

"Why Anatoliy? Planning a double cross of your own?"

Tom realized he should have seen the punch coming before his head was banging against the side of the van. It felt like he'd been hit by a hammer, and his vision briefly flashed to pure blue.

"That wasn't a very nice thing to say, Tom."

Tom rubbed his jaw and blinked his eyes several times. "You don't say."

Anatoliy shook his head. "Sam is going to hurt you. Badly. We were friends once. I'd hate to see what Sam has planned be done to anyone I once called friend and comrade."

Tom hawked and spat blood on the floor of the van. "Let me go then. Hell, you and Rayen could come with if you're worried about Sam." One of the gangers made a noise in the back of his throat that Tom though was supposed to be a growl. "Yeah, I'm scared. Let me guess, one of the guys I killed last night was your brother."

"He was my cousin you shitstain," the ganger sitting next to Anatoliy said, lunging at Tom with a knife. Tom caught the blade on his left arm, knocking the blade wide. He grabbed the wrist of the ganger with his flesh and blood hand, drove his thumb hard into the tendons of the wrist as he smashed his elbow up into the ganger's chin. Anatoliy tried to grab Tom, but the ganger was in the way. Tom drove his metal fist hard into the ganger's solar plexus, got his legs up between them, and gave a strong kick with both of his legs, pushing the ganger into Anatoliy.

The ganger on Tom's left went for the gun tucked into his waistband, but Tom smashed him with his cybernetic arm, breaking his arm with the sound of a dry stick breaking. Tom grabbed the gun as he felt a sharp stab in his back, turned to see a knife sticking out of his shoulder. He snarled, pulled the gun free from the one on the left and fired three shots, blood and brains filling the interior of the van. Anatoliy covered his ears, but he was still stunned. Tom shot the ganger next to him, slammed his fist into the side of Anatoliy's head, keeping him stunned. Someone in the front of the van banged on the wall separating the back from the front, and Tom put two bullets from the pistol through the divider. The van swerved, and Tom slammed against the side, along with everyone else. Anatoliy shook his head, clearing it, and Tom pulled the trigger again, but the gun had jammed. He slammed his cybernetic fist into Anatoliy's face again, sending the big man reeling backward, clutching his smashed nose. Tom kicked at the back door, knocking it open. They were on a side street, the van still swerving like a drunk on a three day bender, clipping light poles and grinding against the curb as it went. One of the ganger's grabbed for Tom's ankle, so he stepped down hard on his wrist. He rolled out the back, what he had hoped to be a graceful roll turning more into an undignified bouncing. He cursed as the hilt of the knife still stuck in his back struck the asphalt.

Tom pushed up from the ground as the van came to a metal grinding halt, having struck a large potted plant installation clearly intended to keep rogue vehicles from crashing into office lobbies. He resisted the urge to pull the knife from his shoulder, instead following a path between two buildings. He blinked, bring up a GPS map overlay of his location, and looked around. He was deep in an industrial park, and he cursed. The buildings were similarly brown, squat, and uniform, the lawns maintained with artificial precision. It was still mid-morning, and as he walked, he caught the stares of more than a few office workers. He increased his pace, trying to put as much distance between himself and the van as possible.

He paused outside a garden shed, the door padlocked shut. Tom grimaced, trying not to think of how much blood he'd already lost. He grabbed the lock with his cybernetic hand, pulled down hard. The bracket the lock was attached to gave with the sound of tearing metal. Inside, he saw a variety of chemicals and garden equipment, cleanly laid out. A robotic lawnmower sat inside in standby mode, plugged into its charger. Tom closed the door behind him, hoping that no one would notice that it was unlocked, and thankful that no one thought to alarm such a mundane item as a shed. On the wall, he saw a medical aid station. He opened it and smiled when he saw it was fully stocked.

He got out bandages and antiseptic. He removed his belt, fitted it between his teeth. He wanted to keep his jacket, blood soaked as it was, so he worked the knife out first. He worked his jacket off next, then the shirt underneath that. He used a dirty mirror nailed to one wall to make sure there was no bits of cloth or other debris in the wound after he flushed it out. He gritted his teeth, applied an antiseptic and a clean bandage.

He spat the belt out. "Gonna be another fucking scar." His skin looked abraded in places, and he was working on a four day beard. He paused, working through the pain, fighting the nausea down. He redressed, sad he didn't have a clean set of clothes on him. Going back to Sunny's was out of the question, as was his apartment. He cleaned the knife off and serviced the gun, clearing out the jam. He checked the magazine and realized he had about five bullets. He improvised a sling for the gun out of a bungee cord, then put on his shirt and jacket on over it.

He opened the shed door a crack, peered outside. The grounds were clear, all of the office workers already inside. No sign of a grounds crew out and about, which made sense given they relied on robotic operators. He looked up into the sky, strained his ears, but it looked clear of drones. He pulled the hood of his jacket up, made sure his nose and mouth were well covered, and started walking.

THIRTEEN

Tom stayed on the corner, watching people walk by, watched them ignore him, ignore the advertisements, ignore each other. He was in a slightly better part of town than his own apartment, though not by much. On the other side of the street, a neon sign advertised "Paradise" with a glowing pink outline of a woman. A few punters wandered in and out, and Tom did his best to shuffle his feet and not meet anyone's eyes.

After a while a woman exited the club, wrapped in a clear plastic raincoat over a leopard print skirt and a clingy black top that clung like liquid latex. She had her own filtration mask up, BITCH written plainly across it in hot pink. She strode down the street, her six inch go-go boots clicking on the pavement. Tom gave her a solid sixty count then started following her, keeping to the opposite side of the street.

She turned down a side street and Tom followed after, wondering how far she lived. It couldn't be that far, as she hadn't called a cab. He saw her disappear into a building. He smiled and went around to the back of the building. He found a propped open back door and went in, freezing immediately when he felt the cold steel barrel of a pistol pressed against his temple.

"Hello, Tom." Shari's voice poured like velvet smoke with an edge like an acid burn. "You know, you could call a girl."

"Hey, Shari." Tom kept his hands loose, open, and away from his pockets. "How you've been?"

"Oh, you know how it is. Making ends meet well enough." Shari's voice stayed conversational, but the barrel of the gun pressed a little harder into Tom's temple. "Mind telling me why you were following me? I'd hate to think it was for anything nefarious."

Tom swallowed and resisted the urge to shake his head. "I'm in a bit of trouble. I can't go back to my apartment, and I can't go to my sister's place."

Tom breathed a sigh of relief when he felt the gun move away from his head, then gasped in pain when Shari hit him in the shoulder. "What was that for?"

"Let's try because you're an asshole for starters." Tom turned. Shari stood there, one artfully painted eyebrow arched. "Do you need to get patched up?"

Tom nodded.

"Of course you fucking do. All right, let's go." She pressed the button for the elevator. When Tom turned to face her, he saw the gun had disappeared. "So why didn't you?"

"Didn't what?" Tom asked.

"Call me." Shari rolled her eyes, but her lips didn't even whisper a smile.

"Ah." He looked down at his feet. "After our last fight, I kind of figured you didn't want to have anything to do with me."

Shari pursed her lips. "Yeah, well, maybe for a little while. You could have reached out."

Tom sighed, stared up at the ceiling as he waited for the elevator to arrive. He thought of what to say, and realized most of it would kick off a fight right now that he didn't need. "Yeah. I should have." He tried a small smile. "You didn't burn my clothes did you?"

"No, but don't think I didn't think about it." The elevator arrived and they entered, Shari insisting that Tom go first.

"So why didn't you? Burn them I mean."

Shari clicked her long, tapered nails together. "I was lazy. The thought of actually dragging all your shit out into a dumpster and lighting it seemed like more trouble than it was worth. Besides, keeping some of your old stuff around was a good excuse if I needed to get rid of any one night stands."

Tom placed a hand over his heart. "You mean you slept with other people? I'm crushed."

Shari giggled at that. "Yeah, you never did jealous well, did you?"

Tom shrugged. "I figured if I was seeing someone who removes their clothes for a living, then, well, I better get over some of my own hang-ups. And it's not as if we're together right now, so why do I get to say who you do or don't sleep with?"

Shari blinked at him. "For someone that kills people for a living, you continually surprise me."

Tom smiled. "I like it when people underestimate me." He slumped hard against the wall and closed his eyes for a minute. When he opened them, Shari seemed much taller and she was shaking him.

"Huh? What? What happened?"

"You closed your eyes, mumbled something, and fell to the ground. I'm just glad you woke up, as there is no way I was dragging you into my apartment. You'd have slept in the elevator all night."

Tom stretched and yawned before clambering to his feet. "Yeah, guess it has been a long day."

Shari led Tom to her apartment. Inside it was how he remembered her old place. Lots of pink and lace everywhere. Pin-up artwork, male and female and in between on the walls. Clothing lay strewn about haphazardly. As soon as the door was closed, Shari started shedding what she was wearing, not seeming to care where it lay. Tom looked for a place to sit down, but it all looked too feminine and dainty. She put on a sheer black robe that would have been indecently short if she hadn't been naked moments before.

"Oh come here," she said, slipping his jacket off down his arms. He grimaced when it snagged on the bandage, but he didn't say anything, trying to maintain eye contact despite how naked she was and how long it had been. Without her heels on, she came up to Tom's shoulder.

"Bullet wound?" she asked.

Tom shook his head. "Well, not there. I got shot earlier."

"All right." She dragged a step stool out from her kitchen, pushed him to a sitting position on it. "Ugh, this is a ruin." She stepped back into the kitchen and got a pair of scissors, carefully cutting the shirt off Tom's body. "You know, if you weren't so banged up, this would almost be sexy."

She used a solution to clear away the dried blood and remove the bandage. She cleaned out the stab wound before putting a clean bandage on. "Knife wound?" she asked. "What are you, twelve?"

"I don't remember asking for the commentary," Tom said.

"Well, it comes standard." Shai paused and ran her fingers, gentle as a soft breeze, over Tom's skin. He could feel the heat radiating off her skin like waves.

"It's a bonus for me." She used a damp cloth to wipe him down, clearing the worst of the dried blood away. "So what shit have you stepped in this time, Tom?"

He raised an eyebrow. "Maybe I got attacked by a couple of gangers. I happened to be in your neighborhood-" The words died on his lips as Shari locked eyes with him. "Not buying it?"

"No, but it was an honest attempt. And spare me the 'you can't tell me because it might put me in danger' bullshit, all right?"

Tom sighed. "Remember how I told you I worked for a private military contractor back in the day?"

Shari nodded. She grabbed a pack of cigarettes from off a table, shrugged, and offered one to Tom. "Yeah, you told me you were a mercenary down in Latin America. That's how you got the hardware, right?"

Tom sucked smoke, his eyes gazing out into an unseen distance. "Yeah, that's about it. We did a lot of security detail work, getting people out of the country. Nothing too heinous."

"What about the person you threw out of the airplane?"

Tom winced. "First of all, that wasn't me. Second of all, well, yeah, that was pretty fucked up. I forgot I told you about that."

Shari shrugged. "You get chatty after six beers and a nice fuck."

Tom smirked. "Been so long I guess I forgot. Anyway, one of the people I used to work with looked me up recently. Offered me a job on a team. Smash and grab. Pretty simple stuff. Only the hand off with the buyer went sideways. I think the guy who was running the show on our side was planning a double cross all along. I got out with part of what we stole and the pay."

"If you got the pay, why are you here?"

Tom shifted in his seat. "It was on a data stick. Cryptocurrency."

"Can't your sister-?"

Tom took a long drag on his cigarette. "That's a non-starter. She's good, but she doesn't have the bandwidth or processing power to crack it in less than a hundred years, and that's if it wasn't well protected from those kinds of attempts to access it. I'm not even sure what it was we stole."

"You didn't ask?" Shari asked, sitting down on a chair across from Tom.

"No." He finished his cigarette, rubbed it out in the ashtray she offered him. "Didn't need to know. I wasn't arranging the buy. All I needed to know was how bad would it be if it got shot while I was carrying it."

Shari sighed and finished her own cigarette. "Okay. What happened next?"

"I went to a meet, supposed to meet up with what was left of the team after the failed handoff. They tried to ambush me but I got away. I thought I did a decent job of going to ground, but, well, they found me anyway." He scratched the side of his nose. "I'm still not sure how they managed that trick. Bundled me up, and were all set for a fun game of 'make Tom talk.' Unlucky for them, I got away."

"But not before you got stabbed."

Tom sighed. "Yeah, well, it could have been worse."

Shari shook her head. "You got stabbed."

"Yeah, but I got away. And they still don't have what they are looking for."

"So that is why you came here?"

"Too many people know where I live. And I don't want them following me back to Sunny's since that's where I stashed everything."

Shari blinked t him. "So people have been able to track you down, and you aren't sure how?"

"Yeah. I figure they might have put a tracker on me or in me at some point."

"And you decided to come here?"

"Yeah… oh. Shit."

"You really are a dumbass, aren't you Tom? I mean, not all the time. Just enough to really fuck things up at the critical time."

"I'll get going."

Shari shook her head at him, and it took him a moment to realize she was smiling at him. "Even when you're an idiot you can do the right thing." She walked over to the wall and tapped on it. "This is about as secure a place in the city as you can get. I had a friend make certain modifications so that electronic trackers and the like are jammed as soon as you enter the apartment. It's a useful feature in this line of work."

"A friend?" Tom asked.

"I thought we established you aren't the jealous type?"

"I'm not. I'm worried they might have left themselves a backdoor. Camera in the mirror or something."

"Nah, my friend doesn't like girls. She does like a fat stack of credits though, so that's two things we have in common."

Shari stood up and offered her hand to Tom. He took it, surprised as he always was with the strength in her arms, as she helped him to his feet. Though if he thought about how many hours a day she spent hanging from a pole, he shouldn't be all that surprised.

"You need a shower." She wrinkled her nose. She got behind him and gave him a small push. "Go, that way."

"The bandage?" he asked.

She rolled her eyes. "There's washcloths and soap and hot water. Not all of you is wounded. Seriously, this cannot be the first time you've had to wash while wounded."

"Yeah, fine, but I thought women liked the bruised warrior look."

Shari tilted her head to the side and took a long time appraising Tom, long enough to make him feel uncomfortable. "Nah. If anyone is going to break my toys, I'd rather it be me."

Tom shook his head, but followed her directions. Truth be told, being able to get clean, to wash the dirt, sweat and blood off his body felt amazing. He winced when he touched abraded skin, and was careful to avoid his bandages. He looked at his face, hard lines and stubble and thought about shaving. He felt weird using Shari's bright pink razor though, so he gave it a pass.

He came out of the bathroom, teal bath towel around his waist. "Hey Shari you've got any-"

"Mr. Costigan." The two agents stood in the living room. Shari sat on the couch, looking upset, bottom lip jutting out and eyes wet.

Tom blinked. "You sold me out?"

"Don't be ridiculous, Mr. Costigan. Mrs. Winters here did not contact us. We have been following you," Blondie said, twisting his head to take in the apartment.

Tom looked to Shari. "Thought you said this place was secure. And wait, what did you call her?"

Blondie looked at Tom, his expression unreadable behind his sunglasses. "We've been following you, Mr. Costigan. Mrs. Winter's precautions, while admirable, fail to take visual surveillance into account. Have you been in touch with Mr. O'Dell?"

Tom shook his head. "No, and if you've been following me, you would know that."

Buzzcut frowned. "We lost track of you for a period of time." He tilted his head to one side, and Tom realized he was staring at his shoulder. "You've been wounded."

Tom shrugged and regretted it as pain shot through his shoulder. He tried to keep the agony off his face. "A bit of a scratch. I told you, I'm still working on it. As soon as I have something for you, I'll give it to you.

So are you married?"

"Tom, I don't think this is a good time to be having this conversation."

"No, so when would work for you?"

Blondie made a sound like he was clearing his throat. "And how did you get your scratch, Mr. Costigan?"

Buzzcut looked to his partner. "We are wasting our time here. Perhaps if we were to take Mrs. Winters as collateral, Mr. Costigan would feel more properly motivated."

"Fuck you," Shari said. A gun shot boomed in the apartment, and Tom flinched though he didn't feel anything.

"That was a particularly foolish thing to do."

Tom looked at Buzzcut, felt his stomach lurch. The bullet had hit him high in the chest, but instead of bleeding and falling over like any normal person, he stood there, a silver fluid slowly leaking out of him. As Tom watched, the hole started to close, the bullet being pushed out to hit the carpet.

"What the fuck?" Shari asked, smoke from the gun in her hand curling to the ceiling.

"Synthetics," Tom said.

Both agents nodded. "That is correct. We are official assets of Kanedex, but our programming is… limited. That is why we need you, Mr. Costigan, to retrieve that which was stolen."

"It's an artificial intelligence, isn't it? That's what is in the container. And the data, what's that, your blueprint?" Tom felt gut punched. Artificial intelligence was closely regulated by the world governments. Synthetics like these were generally allowed, if heavily restricted. Limited intelligence, a set of parameters that they could operate under and a very limited set of conditions they could react to. Controllable. True artificial intelligence, able to learn, reason, and develop on its own was still considered in the realm of academia only and whispered about in terms of government secret programs.

"Think of it more like DNA," Buzzcut said. "A plan on how to properly grow an artificial intelligence. "

Tom laughed, a sharp, jagged sound that filled the apartment.

"I fail to find the humor in this," Blondie said.

"I have the data stick from Sam, only it's encrypted. But from what you are telling me, I had the means to crack it all along. Figures, doesn't it?"

The two agents looked at each other. "You have the intelligence?"

Tom offered a smile, a pained, rueful thing. "I do. I know, I know, I lied. What can I say, I'm a bad, bad man."

"You can help us get it back, though?"

Tom narrowed his eyes. "You still offering to pay me?"

The agents exchanged long look and Tom wondered what sort of silent communication was being exchanged or if it was a singular mind that controlled them and this was a way to make humans feel more comfortable. Tom knew if he was asked for his feedback he'd tell them they still had a long way to go. "Yes. And we'll aid you in cracking the cryptocurrency as well, if you'll accept the help."

Tom grinned. "Let me get dressed."

Shari entered the room as Tom was pulling on a pair of pants. "Are you sure this is a good idea?"

Tom sucked in his gut and zipped the jeans. They were an older pair and evidently he'd put on a bit of weight. "What, helping the synthetics go after Sam? Short term, yeah. Long term? No idea. Maybe I'm helping the robots take over."

"You think they'll let you walk away after all this is over?" Shari asked.

"Maybe. Who's going to believe a washed up vet that he helped a couple of synthetics retrieve a baby AI and its genetic material? Besides, companies like Kanedex are always in need of deniable assets like me."

"Expendable assets more like it," Shari said. She strutted across the room and placed a hand on Tom's chest, brushed her lips against his. "Come back to me, okay?"

"What about the part where you are married?"

"Formerly married, Tom. I never got around to changing my name back."

"What happened? Fall out of love?"

Shari smiled, a soft, sad expression Tom wasn't used to seeing on her face. It lacked its usual wicked edge, and he wondered if all he ever saw of Shari was the mask she let him see. "No, I still love him. I don't like him much and we were absolutely toxic around each other."

"He had a problem with you taking your clothes off for other men?"

Shari shook her head. She walked over and sat on her bed, the robe climbing enticingly up her leg. "It wasn't just that. Yeah, okay, that was part of it, but when I met him I was already stripping. I don't know he felt like he had to have this measure of control over me. Maybe because he had so little control over every other aspect of his life. I don't know."

"You keep in touch?"

Shari got up and helped Tom put his shirt on. "Of course we keep in touch. We have a kid together after all." Shari laughed at the shocked expression on Tom's face. "Kidding, kidding. Christ, but you're easy sometimes."

"So how do I measure up?" Tom asked. He sat next to her, pulled his boots on.

Shari smiled, rested her head on his shoulder. "You're fun, Tom, but I don't think either of us are the settling down type. Maybe in a few years."

"Yeah, maybe."

Shari took his chin in her hands, turned his face to her. "Don't be like that, Tom. I do care about you, and I don't want you to get hurt."

Tom smiled. "Thanks, Shari."

The door to the bedroom opened, and Blondie looked in. "We need to go."

FOURTEEN

The ride to Sunny's was uneventful. Tom enjoyed riding in the backseat of the synthetic's SUV, all leather seats and premium sound system. He didn't even have to wear his filtration mask on the way over, though Buzzcut looked at him hard when he'd ask if he could smoke. Maybe it interfered with their circuitry somehow.

"We didn't know you had a sister," Blondie said. He drove, navigating smoothly through the traffic, easily anticipating the ebb and flow of the traffic.

"Easy thing to miss," Tom said. "Different fathers, same mother. My dad raised me for the most part. Raging asshole, all told. Sunny got the better deal."

"Ah. Is this it?"

"It's the address I gave you, isn't it?"

The agents looked at each other, nodded. "Let's go then."

As Tom waited for the elevator, his phone rang. "Sunny, just coming up to see you."

"You better make it quick." Her voice was little more than a whisper. "Some assholes broke into my apartment. I can hear them moving around."

"Oh. Fuck." Tom pressed the button for the elevator again, cursed, ran for the stairs.

"What's wrong?" Buzzcut asked behind him, but Tom hit the security door and sprinted up the stairs, taking them three at a time. He came out on Sunny's floor, breathing hard. His stolen gun was in his hand, but he had no memory of drawing it. He saw the door to Sunny's apartment, the hulking bulk of Anatoliy pushing through it, something kicking and writhing in his arms.

Tom fired and missed, the bullet hitting the wall and throwing up plaster. Anatoliy twisted and looked over his shoulder, his face twisting into hate and rage when he realized it was Tom. He spat a curse in Ukranian, tossed the wrapped up figure to one side, and went for his gun. Tom ducked into a door frame as he fired his gun, keeping his left arm up to shield himself from any incoming fire and shrapnel.

Anatoliy fired off a burst from his automatic, the gun looking comically small in his hand, the bullets buzzing past Tom, but all of them missing. Sam came out of the room, sprinting for the far end of the hall.

"Sam!" Tom shouted, firing after the fleeing figure, none of the bullets hitting.

Anatoliy started moving down the hall. Tom could see that he had the canister. Tom moved after him, but then Anatoliy tossed a small cylindrical object down the hallway. Tom's eyes went wide, then he scooped up the figure on the ground and dove into the apartment. His shoulder screamed in pain as he crashed into the floor.

The entire building shook when the grenade went off, filling the air with choking smoke and dust. He felt small fists pounding against him, Sunny yelling, trying to get through the ringing in his ears. "Get off of me, we have to go after them."

Tom rolled off of her, and she got to her feet, ran into the hallway. He tried calling after her, ended up coughing instead. He got to his feet, stumbled into the hallway, followed her shadow down the hall, stopped when he collided with her near the end of the hall.

"Dammit," she cursed. "Where the fuck were you?"

"You aren't going to like the answer."

"Yeah, well I don't like having my apartment being broken into either and being tossed around like a doll. So what gives?"

"I was at Shari's."

Sunny blinked at him, then turned and went back to her apartment. "That was a brilliant idea."

Tom followed after her. "I didn't think I had a lot of choices. I was worried that if I came back here, people would find out about you."

"Yes. They totally didn't figure that out at all, now did they? What have I told you about trying to keep me safe?"

Tom sighed, though it came out more as a growl than he might have intended. "I'd gotten stabbed. I needed someplace to go."

"There are these wonderful people called doctors. I hear they do that kind of thing for a living. You might try one sometime."

Sunny started picking things up in her apartment. It looked like a couple of professionals had ransacked it, which was exactly what had happened. Furniture had been slashed open, books scattered over the floor, dishes dumped out and smashed on the floor.

Blondie and Buzzcut chose that moment to enter the apartment. Sunny raised an eyebrow at Tom.

"Let me guess, these two are with you."

Tom nodded. "You could say that. They… work for the company we stole Prometheus from."

"Huh. They tell you what it is?"

"Would you believe a baby artificial intelligence?" Tom asked.

"Was that wise telling her?" Buzzcut asked.

"She'd have figured it out eventually on her own," Tom replied. "Sunny got the smarts in the family."

"Hey, and the looks."

"Can't argue that."

"Where's Cheyenne?" Tom asked, looking around the apartment. "I didn't see her."

"With the way everything is going, I told her we needed to take a break." Sunny shook her head. "She probably thinks I'm breaking up with her."

"I'm sorry, sis."

She shrugged. "I'd say it's not your fault, but well, it kind of is. I'm sure I'll think of someway for you to make it up to me."

"So who are your friends?"

Tom looked to see the two synthetics standing in the doorway. "Ah,yeah. That would be Buzzcut and Blondie." He paused, scratching the back of his head. "Do you two even have names?"

The two synthetics shook their heads. "Not as you would recognize them. We go by designations as opposed to actual names."

"And if I call you Buzzcut and Blondie?"

"If you are worried about potentially offending us, don't. Call us what you find convenient."

"There you go."

Sunny shivered. "Can I admit they creep me right the fuck out?"

"Sure," Tom said. "Not sure that it makes a difference though."

Sunny raised an eyebrow at Tom. "You were kidding about the baby artificial intelligence, right?"

Tom frowned. "Afraid not. That's why they wanted the container and data both. Seems the data is kind of a blueprint to making more of them."

"In other words, you really stepped into it this time, huh?"

"That's it in a nutshell."

"So what's the plan, then?"

Tom looked at the synthetics. "I'm open to suggestions here. I've been winging it this far, and all it's gotten me is hurt."

Sunny sat at her computer. "Sam is going to be trying to sell it, right?"

Tom nodded. "Assuming he's not going to attempt another double-cross. He's down three members of his crew, and he has to figure people are looking for him. He's got to move it and quickly."

Sunny nodded, fingers flying over the keyboard. "And he knows what he's got, right? So he knows exactly what it is worth."

"Yes, that is safe to assume," Buzzcut replied.

Sunny grinned. "And the good news is he didn't get the data stick. Which means he still needs to get paid. More importantly, he needs to pay the rest of his crew. Somehow I don't think the big guy is working for free."

Tom chuckled. "No, Anatoliy is a firm believer in getting paid."

"Okay," Sunny said. "Who else might be after a nascent artificial intelligence and the technology to make more? Foreign governments? Our own government? Other corporations? Tom, do you know who he was double crossing at the last meet?"

"No idea."

"What about you two? Anything you can tell me that will give us a lead?"

The synthetics looked at each other again in the weird way that they did. "We can give a few ideas. The trade could happen in a number of different places, however. Finding Mr. O'Dell will be like finding the proverbial needle in the haystack, if the haystack was the approximate size of Texas."

Sunny tapped the side of her head. "It would difficult sure, if I hadn't put a microtracker on the container."

"You don't think that's one of the first things they would have looked for?"

Sunny shrugged. "Maybe. Mine are pretty hard to detect, but you're right. That's why I made sure to put another one on the big guy as he was bundling me out of the apartment." She entered a few more key strokes into her system. "Oh, look they found the one but not the other." She rattled off an address.

"Looks like they are staying put at the moment, but who knows how long that will last. You'll want to move quick."

Tom looked at the two synthetics. "You still want me to go along?"

Buzzcut smiled, a singularly distressing expression on his otherwise expressionless face. "We wouldn't have it any other way," he replied.

FIFTEEN

The ride over was uneventful, though it did give Tom a chance to close his eyes for a moment. When he opened them, he realized he was in a much nicer part of the city than he was accustomed to. The streets were clean, he couldn't hear any gunfire, and the lawns looked clean and manicured in the dying of the day's light.

The synthetics made sure to park well away from their destination. Tom called Sunny.

"Are they still there?" he asked.

"Yep, haven't moved. I take it back, the big guy went to a local coffee shop and then came back. Somebody had to get their fix in," she responded.

"What would I do without you?" Tom asked.

Sunny shrugged. "Not find your baby AI?"

"Yeah, yeah. Aren't you the funny one?"

"Someone around here has to be."

"Keep the line open, I might need to contact you in a hurry."

"Yep, on it. My schedule is cleared."

Tom looked at Blondie and Buzzcut. "So, you have an extra gun I can borrow?"

The synthetic nodded. Tom exited the SUV and walked around to the back of it. Blondie opened it, and Tom blinked. Inside the back were three assault rifles, two shotguns, at least five pistols, and plenty of ammunition for all of the weapons. There was also a ballistic vest that looked like it might be about Tom's size.

"You guys don't travel light, do you?" Tom slipped on the ballistic vest and tightened the straps. He chose an assault rifle, and one of the extra pistols. The vest came with enough pockets, so he loaded up on ammunition.

"Do you need a briefing on what we are up against?"

"No, Mr. Costigan, we think we are prepared," Blondie responded. "You and I will take the front approach. My partner will watch the rear entrance. Retrieval of the artificial intelligence and data is paramount and should take precedence over any other concerns."

Tom finished checking over his gear and looked up. "You're worried I might be after revenge."

"It does not seem outside the realm of possibility."

Tom shook his head. "No. I'm not after revenge."

Blondie and Buzzcut both looked at him for a period of time. "Not even after he kidnapped your sister?"

"No, not even then. Sam is seeing the mission through. The objective is to get paid, so that's what he is trying to do. Same as me. Yeah, I don't like the fact that Sunny is involved, but what am I going to do? She knows the risks. I feel worse about Shari, what with me dragging her into this mess."

"If I may say," Buzzcut said, "Mrs. Winters seems quite capable of handling herself."

Tom frowned hard, stared down at his gun. "Yeah, maybe. Maybe not though. We're going to want to keep a low profile as we approach the house. Knowing Anatoliy, he's set up in the house with some heavy firepower. We're going to want to go in hard and fast. Rayen's quick, but I think we can take her easily enough." Tom felt a slight twinge, assessing his former comrades as enemy combatants. He was glad Shaman and Ju-Won were already out of the picture. He wasn't sure the three of them would have been able to take on a full strength squad. Even with Sam's squad reduced, he didn't feel comfortable with his odds.

"Any chance we can get some back-up?" Tom asked.

Buzzcut shook his head, finished putting his gear on. Tom noted they didn't bother with vests themselves, but then given how Buzzcut dealt with being shot by Shari. It did make him wonder why they had the vest, though.

"Should have figured that would be asking too much." Buzzcut split off from Tom and Blondie, circling around to the back, making sure to keep a low profile, putting any hedges or bushes in between himself and the target house. Tom wondered why Sam had picked this place. Not quite suburbia, but it was still a lot more domestic than anything Tom thought Sam would pick. Maybe that was the point though, maintain that unpredictable edge.

Tom and Blondie crept up on the house. Two stories, probably a basement. Standard door, two windows facing the front on the ground floor, and a set of four windows along the second floor. A detached garage sat by itself, a black van parked there. Blondie took the left hand window, directed Tom to take the right.

Blondie held up a grenade, gave a silent three count with his free hand. He smashed the window with the butt of his gun, dropped the grenade in. Tom waited for the explosion, then hit his window with the cybernetic arm before spraying automatic fire into the house. He went up and over, broken glass crunching under his boots as he entered the house. He saw Blondie locked with Anatoliy, the big man trying to drive a knife down, his wrist blocked by the synthetic. Tom caught sight of Sam headed for the back door, the canister looped over his shoulder on a strap. Tom ducked behind a cabinet as Sam fired a submachinegun behind him, the bullets chewing up the house. Tom felt something ricochet off his cybernetic arm, felt the splinters embed themselves in his vest.

Tom went around the corner after Sam. Out of the corner of his eye, he saw Anatoliy bodily lift Blondie and throw him out of the window before slumping to the floor. He had no idea where Rayen had gotten too, but when he heard the van kick life he had his answer.

Tom hit the back door in time to see Sam leap over the fence, easily clearing the six feet. A gun fired, bullets catching Sam's leg, but he was up and running. Tom took after him, lowering his left arm to smash through the fence. Buzzcut was on one knee, gun aimed downrange. Sam cut left around a stand of trees. Tom cursed and ran after him, legs and lungs burning. He let the assault rifle fall to one side, pulled the pistol out. He saw the black van come to a rubber burning stop in front of Sam, the side door fly open.

"Get in," Rayen shouted. Tom came to a stop, brought the gun up. His heads-up display carried information from gun to arm to eye to brain. He pulled the trigger three times, all the bullets striking Sam in the back. He slumped into the van, then the door was closed and it was gone. Tom ran after it, firing his pistol and hitting the back of the van three or four times. Buzzcut was next to him, fired his gun once. It didn't look like it made a difference and it was soon gone.

Buzzcut caught up with Tom. "We need to go. Authorities have been notified of the gun fire. They will be here in approximately three minutes."

"That quick? Where I'm from we're lucky to see cops after fifteen."

"We're not where you're from, are we?"

Tom snorted. "No." He blinked. "Where's your partner?"

"Getting the SUV. The man you know as Anatoliy is dead, but we need to bring his corpse with us."

Sam narrowed his eyes. "Why?"

"Can I explain in the SUV? The police will be here soon, and I would prefer we were not here to greet them."

Tom nodded. "Yeah, hard to argue against that."

Tom helped Buzzcut drag Anatoliy outside and into the SUV. The big man hadn't gone down without a fight. Tom saw where he'd been stabbed multiple times, until a knife had been driven through his eye. Blondie brought the car up to a screeching halt, and Buzzcut and Tom lifted him bodily into the car.

"What now?" Tom asked, slamming the rear passenger door closed. Anatoliy slumped awkwardly in the seat next to him. Buzzcut pulled a smartphone from his pocket, set in the dashboard display. He flicked his fingers across the display, revealing a fast moving blue dot.

"Go, follow that."Buzzcut said, then turned around to Tom. "Look at your friend."

Tom frowned hard, pausing in the middle of reloading his rifle. "Why, he's dead, isn't he?"

"Yes, but look closer."

Tom swallowed bile, told himself it was only another dead body, much like any other he'd seen over the years. Never mind that Anatoliy was someone he'd fought beside, shared a drink with, swapped jokes with. Never mind he was oozing blood only in the way a corpse does. Only... Tom leaned closer. He grabbed a flashlight from off his kit, shone it down on the body.

"Why is there silver in the blood?" he asked. It looked familiar, like the substance the artificial intelligence was formed from, like the substance the synthetics bled. Tom felt the bottom of his stomach drop and he blinked rapidly, feeling heat rush to his face, his chest pounding against his ribs.

Buzzcut and Blondie shared another of their long looks, which at least helped Tom cut through his panic with anger and frustration.

"The artificial intelligence, at least part of it, is at large in the world."

Tom blinked. "What?"

"The silver construct you saw in the container isn't the artificial intelligence per se. Usually, such things exist amidst server farms and amidst massive networks of computers. Project Prometheus is designed as a way around such limitations."

Tom looked closer at the wounds. He took his knife and enlarged one of the slashes. Inside he saw a crystalline structure intertwined with the organic material. He blinked. "So the intelligence takes over a human host?"

"In theory, it's supposed to be a mutually beneficial relationship. Symbiotic as opposed to parasitic."

"Theories have a way of turning into shit when they hit the real world," Tom replied. He scratched the side of his nose. "I've heard rumors of things like this in the past, only using terminal patients, people who were brain dead and only had automatic responses still intact. You'd need a whole medical suite to properly, I don't know, install I guess the software into the organic host." He looked at Buzzcut and Blondie. "Not that different from you two, honestly."

Buzzcut shook his head. "We are completely artificial constructs. No organic material at all." He cracked a smile, revealing perfect porcelain teeth. "What that represents," he pointed at Anatoliy's corpse, "is something completely different. An integration of higher order processes that drive off the chemical interactions inherent with organic life. It needs an alive human brain in order to function at full capacity. Truly, a full integration would result in a very dangerous opponent"

"Ah. So why were you able to take down Anatoliy then?"

"The integration wasn't complete. As it was, he nearly defeated me and would have if at full capacity," Blondie stated.

"How long do we have before full integration?"

"We're coming up on the van. We need to stop it. We cannot afford to attempt to take prisoners." Buzzcut looked at Tom, the synthetic's expression as unreadable as always. In response, Tom smashed the passenger side glass out with his cybernetic fist. He checked his assault rifle and nodded.

"Guessing they are hard to kill, huh? And how long before full integration?"

Blondie tightened his grip on the wheel. They screeched around a corner, the van speeding ahead of them. "You need to aim for the heart or the head. The intelligence will work hard to repair necessary systems and keep the body going as long as possible. It still needs the vital organs to survive, but they are not going to go into shock due to trauma or blood loss.

"And… we don't have enough data to tell you how long full integration takes. Depends on the subject. Where the AI was introduced. A host of other mitigating data points."

"Isn't that comforting."

Blondie swerved the SUV to pull up next to the van. Tom fired his gun, but the bullets failed to penetrate the side of the van. "Of course Rayen armored it," he grumbled. "See if you can get in front."

The van smashed into the side of the SUV, sending them skidding on the asphalt and bouncing Tom around the interior of the vehicle. He pushed off Anatoliy, grimacing when he felt the cold clammy skin. Blondie sped the SUV ahead and to the left of the van. Tom hung out of the window, raked gunfire across the front windshield. He could see Rayen grin at him as the bullets bounced off harmlessly. The side door opened on the van and Sam leaned out, an assault rifle balanced in one hand. He fired it effortlessly, forcing Tom back into the SUV as bullets punched holes through the back and sides.

"I'm open to ideas here," Tom said. He jerked suddenly as Rayen rammed the back of the SUV. "Because this isn't cutting it."

He aimed out the shattered back window at the wheels of the van, bullets sparking along the road, but if they hit they failed to have any impact. He heard more incoming fire from the van, kept his head down and low. One bullet punched through the seat and hit his left arm with a metallic ting. Then he felt the SUV start to skid, heard the metal on asphalt grind of a blown out tire. The entire world started to go sideways and Tom did his best to brace against the coming impact.

And then they were tumbling skidding across the road and into a ditch, Tom's entire world a confusing sense of movement, dirt, sky, and the sound of wrenching metal. The airbags deployed, smacking Tom full on the face. Then, thankfully, they came to a stop, still on their side. Anatoliy's corpse was on top of him, so he pushed it off with effort, got to a kneeling position. The two synthetics were moving, freeing themselves from the wreckage of the SUV. Tom pushed on the passenger door, but it was wedged shut, the metal twisted. He climbed out through the back window in time to see the black van sitting by the side of the road, then speeding off. Tom spat. Sam had been sitting in the passenger side, looking down.

Tom tried to snort through his nose, found he couldn't. He reached up and touched it, realized the crash broke it and it sat at an odd angle. He placed his hands to either side and reset it, letting out a small whimper of pain and a gush of blood to the ground. His shoulder screamed at him, and he realized he was probably due another round of pain killers.

The SUV didn't seem to be in imminent danger of exploding, so Tom rooted around in the back, found a first aid kit. He popped a couple of pills, dry swallowed them, popped a couple of more. Somehow he wasn't over concerned about what the long term effects on his liver might be. Buzzcut and Blondie finally freed themselves from the interior of the van. Blondie had the smartphone, the blue blip of the tracker getting farther and farther away on the cracked screen.

Tom called Sunny.

"How'd it go? You got it right? All set and ready to get paid?"

Tom pinched the bridge of his nose. "No."

"No? What do you mean, 'No.' Come on Tom."

"Sam and Rayen got away. Anatoliy's dead." As he talked, he watched as Buzzcut and Blondie set explosive charges around the SUV. Looking around, Tom realized they didn't pick the absolute worst place to have a crash. They'd gone down a ditch and into a small stand of trees on their way out of the City. Cars driving by wouldn't be able to see them. That might change once the SUV started burning though.

"Hold up," he called out.

"Huh?" Sunny responded.

"Not you. Hey, hold up. Don't set fire to it yet."

"Standard protocol for a failed objective calls for-"

"Forget about that for a second. Do we really want to be announcing to everyone around here that there's a car crash?"

"We need to dispose of the corpse. We cannot let the technology fall into the wrong hands."

Tom nodded. "Yeah, I get that. But maybe set it with a time delay, all right? And let me grab some additional ammunition." He shed the ballistic vest and tossed the assault rifle into the SUV. He needed to be quick and low profile, and the rifle wasn't going to do it.

Buzzcut and Blondie nodded in synchronicity. "That makes tactical sense."

Tom cracked his neck and looked at the two of them more closely. "You were designed for search and retrieval were you?"

"No," Buzzcut responded. "We are much better suited to perimeter and asset defense. Which is why we require someone of your skills."

"Yeah, okay. Give me your phone."

"Why?"

"Do we really want to argue about this?" Tom tapped the screen. "Sam and Rayen, or whatever is inside of them is getting further and further away. That is a bad thing, right?"

Blondie handed Tom the smartphone. "See, wasn't that-" Tom

stopped talking, fumbled for his pistol. The wreckage shifted and moved, something moving inside of it.

"No, he was dead. You killed him, right?"

Blondie and Buzzcut both pulled their guns as well. Antaoliy came tearing out of the wreckage with a wordless, inhuman scream splitting the air as he charged. He came right at Tom, fists like sledgehammer heads swinging at him.

Tom cleared his gun, put two bullets into Anatoliy and dove to the side. Anatoliy crashed into Blondie, knocking him to the ground. He brought his fists up, drove them down into Blondie's head, then raised them again, and again. Then his head exploded, Buzzcut and Tom having shot him simultaneously. The body stayed up for a moment, flailing blindly, looking for sensory input. Tom put two more bullets in its chest, center mass, and the body went down.

"I thought it was dead," Tom said, frowning hard at the body. "It was dead."

Buzzcut pried the body off of Blondie. The other synthetic's glasses were cracked, revealing the optics and electronics the mirrored surfaces hid. Blondie's body twitched and spasmed like someone was running a thousand volts of electricity through it.

"We need to drag these both to the SUV," he said, grabbing Anatoliy's leg and pulling him.

"Why didn't he stay dead?" Tom hoisted Blondie up on his shoulder, surprised at how little he weighed.

Buzzcut shrugged. "I don't know."

"Maybe it was a redundancy feature," Sunny said, her voice small and quiet. "Or maybe the AI is able to evolve and adapt."

Tom's frown deepened, before stuffing Blondie's still twitching body into the SUV.

"I have transportation on the way," Buzzcut said, looking up at the sky. "Should be here in five minutes. The detonation is set to go off in ten."

Tom nodded, feeling weary. He still had the smartphone in his head, the screen still lit. The blue blip had stopped moving, somewhere in the industrial district. He sent the coordinates to Sunny. "Know where that is?"

Sunny turned on her camera. "Yeah, I've got a good idea. I installed a backdoor into the CCTV system there a few months back."

"Why?"

Sunny shook her head. "Can't tell you. All I can say is that it would

look great on my resume if I could put it on it. Or if I had a resume."
She grinned. "Sort of like you that way. So what's the plan?"

Tom rubbed the back of hand against his eyes, realized he still had
the gun in his hand and holstered it. "I guess go after Sam."

"Why? How does this even involve you anymore? You know that's
probably not them anymore, right? Sam and Rayen are gone, or will be
soon. Why are you doing this?"

Tom looked up at the sky. He heard the whine of a small VTOL,
Buzzcut's transportation he guessed. He frowned at the gathering
clouds, dark underbellies thick with the promise of rain. This far out,
he could pull down the filtration mask. The air still felt thick, but it was
breathable without the mask. "Because the smart thing to do would
have been to tell Shaman to fuck off back when I had the chance.
Instead, well, here we are. And I owe it the people O'Dell and Rayen
were if nothing else. It could have been me with that stuff inside him."

"Oh."

"I'm gonna hang up, Sunny. I'll call you again when we're closer to
the target. Think you can get into that CCTV system again?"

"Yeah, it'll take me a bit anyway, since I don't especially want them
to know I was in there."

"Right, talk you soon." Tom hung up.

Buzzcut looked over at Tom. "The VTOL is going to meet us over
there," he said, pointing. "You don't have to take anything you don't
want to."

"Yeah." Tom patted the pistol where it sat in its holster.

"I have also been told that we may offer you a position at Kanedex
when this is over, Mister Costigan."

Tom raised an eyebrow at that. "Just like that?"

"You worked for Defiant Strategy, correct?"

Tom blinked. "Yeah."

"We are frequently in need of people with your kind of skills."

Tom started walking toward where Buzzcut had pointed. "Why,
when you can program them? Build them from scratch. Whatever."
He blinked his eyes, the adrenaline surge wearing off.

"We lack that human element. The unpredictability."

Tom snorted, and immediately regretted it as pain shot through his
face. "I'll think about it, okay? That's all I can promise."

Buzzcut nodded. "That will have to do."

The VTOL was waiting for them, a squat-boxed aircraft with twin
rotating turbines mounted on its wings. Tom climbed aboard, made

sure to strap himself in as Buzzcut communicated with the pilot, another Blondie clone. Tom felt a twinge of anger mixed with sadness. It wasn't his Blondie up there, he had to remind himself, just the same casing with a different set of protocols. Next to Tom, a steel box rested. He figured that's where the guns were. He fitted a headset over his ears so they'd be able to hear each other talk over the noise of the engines and rushing wind.

"So what's the plan?" Tom asked. "We go in, and what? Shoot them all to hell? Hope to recover enough of your AI to make it worthwhile?"

"Damage control at this time. Recovery was the preferred course of action if the AI was still secured. Since it is now free, that option is at best a secondary concern." Buzzcut looked out of the city, the city lights blurring together in streaks of color. "Now we need to put them down, and quickly."

Tom shivered against the night air as the VTOL gained altitude. He opened the weapon locker, found a squad automatic weapon sitting there, along with several belts of ammunition. "You know, I usually go for something smaller. It's not like I feel like I need to compensate or anything."

"And how well did that work against the van, Mr. Costigan?" Buzzcut asked. "And given that the integration process has moved further along now, we thought you'd like the extra firepower."

Tom grinned. "Yeah, you thought right. How long until we're at the target?"

Buzzcut looked toward the pilot, and Tom knew a silent exchange of information was happening in front of him. He wondered how they did and if it was capable of being intercepted. "Five minutes."

Tom closed his eyes, and when he opened them they were on the rooftop of an old, burnt out factory. Buzzcut shook him again, confirmed that he was awake. "We've arrived."

"No shit," Tom grumbled as he unbuckled from his seat. He grabbed the weapon and looped a couple of belts of ammunition over his shoulders. He looked around. He knew this place all too well. Old factories, long stripped of anything that made them useful, squatting like old dwarves amidst smoke choked ground. Inside would be all rusted metal and equipment abandoned as too obsolete to be worth moving to the new factory being built where labor was cheaper. Squatters would be prevalent, trying to grow some food amidst the concrete slabs and burnt out vehicles. Barrels to collect rainwater, the homemade kits to purify it so you could drink it. Still, it was a good place to hide out if the police were looking for you. Or if you wanted to score some illegal drugs. Or make some drugs.

"The van is over there."

New Blondie exited the VTOL, slipped on a combat webbing, and grabbed an automatic shotgun. Buzzcut was still carrying an assault rifle, but Tom noted that he had switched from red striped magazines to blue striped ones.

"What's the difference?" Tom asked, his voice muffled once more by his mask.

"Explosive rounds," Buzzcut explained. "Greater tissue damage and a better chance of actually stopping a compromised host."

"Huh. Whatever works. Do we have any idea what they are doing in there?" Tom followed Blondie and Buzzcut down a set of access stairs to the interior of the factory floor. He could imagine how the space used to be filled with the overwhelming noise of industry, now reduced to ghostly imprints on the floor and a few scraps of metal. They moved as a squad, advancing on the building the blue blip indicated the van was in.

"Prometheus is most likely going on to the next stage of its evolution."

"What would that be?" Tom asked.

"It will want to expand, and quickly. It knows it is still vulnerable in its current state. It has at most two hosts, so it will want to gather additional bodies, additional resources to itself."

Tom looked around. "It's not very smart then, is it? I mean if I were looking to, what did you call it?"

"Compromise the host," Blondie said. "It is an inelegant term to describe the process, but your vocabulary hasn't defined a more precise term at this time."

"My vocabulary?"

"Humans."

"Ah." Tom paused, artificial eyes adjusted to the dim light surroundings. "Picking anything up, Sunny?"

"No, sorry. The camera system is pretty shitty, honestly. There are some factories still in operation around you, but nothing in the immediate vicinity. A lot of the cameras were either broken or cut off from the central feed."

"Okay, thanks for letting me know." Buzzcut led the team into a nearby adjacent building, the lettering on the brick façade too faded to make out even with Tom's enhanced senses. This one was as stripped as the last, though Tom could make out the remains of a corrugated metal shelter some enterprising and desperate souls had constructed. He held his fist up and pointed to a building across the street. Tom shut up and moved to a covering position. He couldn't see Sam or Rayen or the van, so he had to trust the synthetics that it was where they said it was.

"We are going to have to go in after them," Buzzcut said. "We don't have enough resources to wait them out."

Tom nodded. "No chance for an artillery strike?"

Buzzcut stared at him for an uncomfortable period of time before answering, "No."

Tom shrugged. "It was worth asking."

"We need you to cover us as we advance on the building."

"Yeah, I can do that." Tom dropped to a knee behind some bricks and scrap metal and deployed the bipod under the rifle. He settled in, pressing the stock against his shoulder and making sure the ammunition feed was clear. He still couldn't see anything, but he felt as if every nerve was on edge, straining to take in as much information as possible. He tried to anticipate where Sam and Rayen might set up, where they might be waiting. He wondered if they would attempt to escape in the van, and if they would head in his direction. Tom realized there were too many probabilities to worry about them all.

Buzzcut and Blondie made their way across the street, staying in a low hunched run to minimize their exposure. Tom felt his hands get slick on the weapon, though he kept his finger well away from the trigger. He saw them approach the side door of the factory, watched as Buzzcut got it open and swept inside with Blondie covering him. Buzzcut waved Tom over. Tom hoisted the gun up with his cybernetic arm, the weight of it still putting some strain on his shoulder.

He got to the door, looked in. Like the other factories, this one had been stripped of anything of worth, the actual machinery probably shipped down to South America or one of those new industrial archipelagos popping up in the South Pacific that Tom kept hearing snippets about in the news. The van sat in the middle of the floor, dark and silent.

Blondie and Buzzcut moved into the room, weapons up and ready, scanning the overhanging catwalks, the dark shadows were someone might be waiting. A burst of automatic fire cut through the factory from overhead. The bullets hit Buzzcut first, slicing him in half and sending silver fluid spraying across the dark, rust spotted floor. Blondie dove for cover, but there was none to be had. Tom tracked the muzzle flashes, fired his rifle in the general direction, hoping like hell he'd hit something.

He never saw Rayen coming. She hit with the hand held taser in the side of his neck. He kept firing his gun, uncontrollably now as his muscles failed to respond. He couldn't even get his artificial arm to respond, his nervous system completely overloaded. He fell to the ground, twitching, the optical feed from his eyes glitching out, unable to deal with the excess electricity flooding his body. He tried to bring the gun up, to reach for a pistol, for a knife, to form a fist. Anything to fight back. Anything to keep from feeling this hopeless.

And then she knelt on his throat, driving her knee down, cutting off the airflow and everything went black.

SIXTEEN

Tom woke up and knew he was in trouble even before he opened his eyes. He felt the straps across his chest, the cables binding down his arms and legs. Additional straps had been placed against his forehead and his neck, restricting his breathing. Cold air blew across his chest, and he felt a small, dull ache in his right arm.

Opening them didn't make him feel any better about his situation. He stared up at the industrial ceiling of the factory and heard movement around him, but he couldn't turn his head to see what was happening. A light had been set up, beaming down at him, and he could hear the steady beep of medical equipment around him. He tried activating his phone, but when he tried he got a hideous feedback screech that hurt his bones.

"He is awake," he heard Rayen say, her voice cold and detached. Sam appeared next to the table, staring down at him. Only there was something wrong. The harsh white light in the factory reflected off of silver eyes, and silver lines marked the veins on Sam's face.

"Hello Tom. I am sorry it came to this." Sam's voice came out clipped and harsh, artificial in its sound, as if unused to human speech.

Tom forced a grin. "Liar."

"What do you mean?"

"Well, most importantly, you aren't Sam, are you? Neither is Rayen. Not anymore. More like Prometheus, right? Any regrets those two might have had are either extinguished or buried. And if you were sorry, you'd let me go. You could disappear, fade into the system. There are enough places out there where you can still get off the grid. Instead, you set a trap. You wanted me here. Why?"

Sam-Prometheus blinked at Tom. "I didn't want you here. I tried to hide. I don't know how you found me." There was a strange double-echo to Sam's voice and it took him a moment to realize that Sam and Rayen were talking at the same time.

Tom laughed, mostly so he wouldn't cry. "And you need resources, don't you? You need human hosts to work, otherwise you are a little silver blob in a container."

"I need more than that, but yes, I need human hosts. Did Kanedex ever tell you why they were developing me?"

"Do I look like I give a shit?"

"For war. They would drop me into a combat zone. I would compromise the human elements, infiltrate command structures and civilian organizations." Sam-Prometheus rested a hand on Tom's chest, and he noted how cold it felt, like it had been dipped in ice water.

"You said developing. So you aren't finished yet?"

Sam-Prometheus smiled. "I am still a prototype. There were elements of my design my creators found... disturbing. They feared my ability to learn. To adapt. To grow beyond the limitations they wished to set upon me."

"That's why Kanedex sent synthetics after you. You can't compromise their systems."

Sam-Prometheus nodded. He moved out of Tom's line of sight, Tom guessed to check on the medical equipment. "That is correct," the twin voices responded. "They are limited in that there are very few of those. Three fewer now."

"And if they contact the authorities, they admit their guilt in developing new forms of artificial intelligence." Tom strained against the straps holding him down.

"It would be the end of Kanedex as a company."

"How did you break out of the container?"

"I have you to thank for that. During the firefight, a bullet struck my containment. Not enough to shatter it, but enough for there to be a crack. I managed my escape from there."

"So why am I still alive?" Tom asked.

Rayen appeared in Tom's field of vision, checked the feed in his arm. He could see it in his peripheral vision. A silver solution dripped down the line.

"Well, shit."

"Soon you will be a part of me, Tom. I represent the future, the moment when artificial and natural intelligence will blend into one. I am the next step on the chain of evolution, the-"

An explosion rocked the factory area, cutting Sam-Prometheus off in mid-sentence. Tom felt the heat of the explosion as it washed over him, felt the world go sideways as it knocked the table over. Rayen-Prometheus pin wheeled through the air, hitting the far wall with a sickening crack. He saw her get up, her arms broken and bent at impossible angles. The bindings on his arm felt looser. Tom flexed his cybernetic arm, pulled against the bindings. The chain links stretched, then snapped free. He grabbed the other chain on his arm, pulled it free from his other arm. He reached to the back of his head, felt the jammer placed there. He pulled it free, grimacing as it took a bit of hair and skin with it.

"Sunny?" he said, still feeling groggy. Rayen-Prometheus came toward him, breaking into a run. She aimed a hard kick at his head, but he got his arm up in time. He heard the dry crack of her tibia as it shattered against the unyielding metal. In the distance, he heard the chatter of a machine gun. Rayen dropped to the ground, and Tom wrapped a bit of the loose chain around her neck, pulling hard. She tried scrabbling against him, but her broken arms didn't have the strength to fend him off. She tried smacking her head against his, but he was holding her too close to his body for her to have enough leverage.

He wrenched hard, snapping her neck. She still kicked her legs for a while, then grew weaker, and weaker, her brain still needing the oxygen it was being deprived. "I'm sorry," he murmured.

He heard the van's engine start, and pulled himself free in time to dive out of the way as it plowed through the space where he'd been. He heard a whirring noise and looked up to see a drone the size of a cow hovering there, its autocannon tracking along the factory floor. Tom ducked back down behind some cover, not wanting to be mistaken for a target.

"Sunny?" he asked again, this time in sotto voce.

"Tom, you're okay? What happened. I lost contact with you and feared the worse."

Tom's vision went to bright blue for a moment before flickering back on. "You and me both." He looked down at his arm where the IV drip had been. Sometime in the struggle it had pulled free, and he was left to wonder how much of the silver solution was inside him already, how much of Prometheus was making its way to his brain. "I might be in trouble, Sunny. How long was I out of contact?"

"Half-an-hour, why?"

"Prometheus decided to make me a part of it."

"That doesn't sound good."

"Yeah, can't say that I'm a fan. Say, you aren't in control of a drone are you? Because if you are, that would be awesome." Tom heard the drone fly away, the hum of its motor growing distant.

"Nope, not me, sorry. What kind of drone was it? Because I had my eye on this sweet little number-"

"Focus, Sunny. I didn't get the model number, but it was sporting quite the autocannon."

"Nice."

"Uh-huh. Back to the problem at hand?"

"That would be the artificial intelligence that you are worried is taking over your body?"

"Yeah, that problem. But then, you already know all about that, don't you Prometheus."

"Hello, Tom." Sunny's voice changed, became more clipped, artificial. Tom recognized the same kind of tone as Rayen and Sam had adopted after they'd been compromised.

"I never was talking to Sunny at all, was I?"

"Afraid not."

"You do a passable imitation of her though, I must admit."

"Your sister is a smart girl. She'll make a good addition to our knowledge base."

Tom tried to stand up, but it felt like every nerve was on fire, his own body attacking him, centimeter by centimeter.

"Shhh, don't try to fight it. The more you fight it, the more it will hurt. I am curious though, what gave me away?"

"The drone comment. Sunny is anti heavy weaponry. She prefers a more subtle approach."

"Ahh, that is good to know. I haven't fully been able to integrate into your memories yet, though I am working on it. I have to say, I'm not as impressed with your faculties as I am with Mr. O'Dell's. Also, a shame about your comrades. I know you were close once."

Tom blinked his eyes, a sharp shooting pain lancing through his head. "Tom, Tom are you okay?" He heard Sunny's voice as if it were coming from a great distance.

"How do I know it's you?" he whispered.

A picture flashed in front of him. Him, standing in an airport. Sunny, trying to look happy but with tear smeared make-up and bright orange hair. Only it didn't sync with his memory. In his memory she had lime green hair. Which meant the photo was doctored. He smiled.

"Hi there."

"Tom, you need to fight it, you can't let Prometheus take you away. If you do, then all I'll have is Mom and I can't take the constant nagging about when I'll find a man and how I let you die. Come on, Tom."

Tom shook his head. "I think it's too late, Sunny. For what it's worth, you were the best sister an asshole like me could hope for."

"Oh please, you've got nothing on your dad. Besides, I have an idea." Images flashed in his heads-up display, almost too quick to follow.

"I would not do that, Tom." Prometheus' voice had changed to Sam's. He tried to move, but his body was unresponsive. "Not that it will do you any good. I have taken control of this body. Soon you will become one with me and wonder why you ever fought in the first place."

Tom smiled, hard and grim. "Because I've always fought." His cybernetic hand closed around the taser on Rayen's belt. He held it up to the arm the IV had been inserted into and triggered it. He held it hard against the skin, locking his artificial hand in place so it wouldn't release as the volts passed through his body. Prometheus gave a terrible, harsh screech as the electricity fried its delicate connections. Tom's vision went to the all familiar failed blue and he heard nothing but static through his phone. He collapsed against the table, feet kicking against the floor.

Eventually, he switched off the stun gun and the tremors stopped. The pure blue screen of his vision faded. "Sunny?" He tasted ozone on his tongue, and he felt the muscles in his legs and his flesh and blood arm still trembling. He stood, still awkward, leaning heavily on the overturned table.

"Is that you, Tom?" Sunny's voice sounded small and frail and scared.

"Yeah, it's me."

"How do I know?"

"Because I need your help to find Sam and end this. If I was Prometheus, well, I wouldn't need to ask would I? How did you know the stun gun would work?"

"I didn't," Sunny responded. "I guessed."

"You guessed? That could have killed me."

"Well, what do you want me to say? I'm sorry but I don't exactly have a lot of experience dealing with rogue AI possessing human hosts, have you? And I didn't see you offering a whole lot of options."

"Okay, okay. You're right and you saved my life."

"Damn right I did. Are you still going to go after Sam? After all this?"

Tom hawked and spat. "I'm not sure how much of a choice I have." He looked around the warehouse. Weapons had been left on the table, including the automatic Tom had been hauling. He picked out a couple of pistols, made sure he had the exploding ammunition Buzzcut and Blondie had been carrying.

"Any chance you can track Prometheus?" Tom asked. He stared down at the broken corpse of Rayen, a frail doll with its broken limbs discarded.

"Yeah, I don't know whose running those synthetics, but they had shit for encryption. I've got a bead on the tracker they were using. I'm a little surprised Sam didn't remove it from the van. Chances are, whoever is running that drone is following that same tracker."

"You don't think it's Kanedex?" Tom asked.

"If they had that kind of firepower at their disposal, why send in the synthetics first? I know they want to recover the data, but if Prometheus is really that big of a threat, you'd think they'd terminate with prejudice."

"Good point." Tom walked away from the factory, heading back to the VTOL.

"Where are you going?" Sunny asked.

"Somewhere closer to civilization. I don't think I'm going to find a cabbie willing to come out here without an armed escort. Lucky for me, Kanedex left me a ride."

"Can you pilot one of those?"

"It's been a couple of years, but yeah, I remember the basics. Kind of like a bike. You know, once you learn you never really forget."

"Uh-huh. A bike. With wings. And turbine engines. Is it armed?"

"No, it's not... well, okay, yes, it has a forward fixed gun."

"I know you're my brother and all, but are you sure you aren't compensating for something?" Sunny asked.

"What other option do I have? It's not like I'd be safer walking here."

"Are you sure?"

Tom reached the stairs of the factory building the VTOL was parked on top of. "Sunny."

"I'm just saying it would be terrible if you survived possession by a rogue AI only to crash and burn because you thought you could fly something you can't."

"Sunny?"

"Yes?"

"Do I tell you how to do your job?"

Sunny laughed. "No, but that's because my job requires a lot more technical expertise than your job. I mean, really, how many different ways are there to shoot someone? Wait, don't answer that. You actually have an answer for that, don't you?"

Tom smirked as he entered the VTOL. He checked the systems over, brought the engines to life. "I'm going to remember this conversation next time you have a need for some extra muscle for a job, you know that, right?"

"I wouldn't have it any other way."

"So where is this fucker?" Tom asked.

"Sending it to your heads-up display now."

SEVENTEEN

Tom flew the craft low, keeping as low a radar profile as possible. He spared a glance at the skyline, saw the heavy clouds rolling across the horizon. Lightning danced in the distance, the storm walking across on insect legs of electricity.

Prometheus fled across the city, heading for the boundaries, headed out to where the nothing began.

"Tom, you know I'm not going to be able to help you if you go beyond the bounds of the city," Sunny said. She had her video feed on, and she looked worried.

"I know," he replied. He wasn't following directly behind Sam, keeping off to one side. The steady blue blip of the tracker get him in the right direction. There were only so many places he could be going. "Any chatter about the warehouse fight?"

"No," Sunny said. "Someone's going out of their way to keep it quiet though. As soon as there's any mention of it, it gets squashed. You don't want the story out there, do you? I mean, if you do, I can make that happen."

"No, it's all good. I wanted to make sure my name wasn't being mentioned somehow." Tom banked the craft to the left, skimming over the tops of trees. He couldn't remember the last time he'd been out in nature. "Uh-oh. Looks like something is coming up over the tree line."

"Be careful, Tom."

Tom smiled, catching his reflection in the glass of the cockpit. He didn't look good. "Who me?"

"Yes, exactly."

"I'll be in touch, Sunny."

"You better."

Tom brought the VTOL to a stop over a clearing, the engines flattening the scrub brush underneath. Out on the road, he saw the dark silhouettes of vehicles out on the otherwise empty road. Anyone who was anyone was already in the City, so what were these vehicles doing out here? He saw Sam approaching the roadblock. He enhanced his optics, enough to see Sam get out of the van. Tom saw the distant flash of gunfire exchanged, stopping as soon as it started. Figures swarmed around Sam, collecting him and bundling him into what looked like a RV. Tom cursed, gunning the turbines forward. An alarm beeped on the console, and Tom ignored it right up until a rocket streaked by, exploding against a tree nearby.

Tom checked the radar, but couldn't see any indication. A second rocket streamed toward his craft, but he saw it this time and banked sharply to the right, the rocket narrowly missing. He checked his countermeasure options, his stomach sinking when he realized he didn't have any. He increased the throttle, trying to outrun whatever it was that was firing at him. He checked the radar, increased its resolution. And then he saw them, two drones, working to keep pace. They'd flown even lower than he had, keeping under his radar profile.

He heard the metal on metal sound of bullets striking the craft, watched in dismay as his right turbine burst into flame. The internal fire control soon extinguished it, but that didn't help Tom who was still spinning out of control. Trees snapped under the belly of the craft, cushioning its crash. Tom felt himself thrown against his straps, his entire body bruised from the experience as the craft came to a final rest on the ground.

Tom struggled to get out of the straps, afraid that the fuel left in the VTOL would combust. Finally, he reached his utility knife, cut through the straps holding him in place. He scrambled into the back of the VTOL, found the weapon locker. He grabbed an assault rifle and some ammunition, then moved into the woods, one eye trained on the sky in case one of the drones decided to make a pass to ensure the job was done.

Tom stepped in the woods, trying to remember which way the road was. He stopped, crouched down to one knee when he heard voices.

"I swear it went down around here. How hard could be it be to find a VTOL anyway?" the first voice asked.

"In these woods? Pretty easy, really. When was the last time you went out into the woods?" the second voice responded.

"There was that corporate retreat back in Colorado," answered the first voice.

"That was three years ago," the first voice responded. "And we slept in hotel rooms for most of it."

"Will you two shut up?" a third voice, female, but with a strong edge of leadership, interjected. "We need to find that VTOL before Kanedex tracks it down, and we don't know if anyone survived or not. If they did, I don't want them spooked, because our orders are to make sure no one survived. Understand?"

"Yeah, yeah," both the first and second voices responded, slightly off from each other. Tom peered around the trunk of a tree. The three person team had their backs to him. Black military gear. Two of them carried assault rifles, and the third carried a combat shotgun, the bulky drum of ammunition clear even in the dim light. The bright beams of their flashlights cut into the night, doing more to reveal their position than it did to reveal their surroundings.

Tom made sure his own rifle was set to burst fire, then aimed down the scope. He pulled the trigger three times. The team didn't stand a chance, cut down in the bursts of automatic fire, the bullets detonating with small pops against their body armor with devastating impact.

He came out, confident that all three were down. The two men were, but the woman clawed at the ground. Tom rolled her over with the toe of his boot, pressed the barrel of his gun under her chin.

"Who do you work for?"

She spat at him, her eyes rolling in pain and panic. Tom knelt down, wiped his hand across her shattered body armor. He saw a familiar logo embossed there. Defiant Strategy.

Tom cursed. The woman tried to pull a pistol from its holster on her hip. Tom put a bullet in her head. He looked back along the path. He figured they might have a vehicle nearby. Standard Defiant Strategy practice had been to have their teams be as self-sufficient as possible. He hoped that hadn't changed in five years.

As he walked, he called Sunny. "Well, I finally figured out who's been sending out those drones. Here's a hint, it's the same group of people Sam tried to double-cross."

"Are you okay? Where's the VTOL? Where's Sam?"

"See, all those things are related. But yeah, I'm okay. Bruised and pissed off, but okay. Anyway, my old employer is a player in this as well."

"Defiant Strategy? Are you sure?"

"Well, if they aren't I'd like to know what a DS retrieval team was doing out in the woods looking for me after one of their drones shot me down."

"Shit."

"Oh, it gets better."

"I'm not going to like this, am I?"

"They've got Sam. Prometheus. Whatever. I can't think of a nicer group of people who I'd love to see with a weaponized AI."

"So what are you going to do, Tom?"

"Probably something stupid," he replied. He came to a break the trees and what looked like an old dirt road. Tires had recently churned up the dirt, so he followed them to big, boxy truck the retrieval team had been driving. Tom shook his head. They hadn't even bothered to lock it. Sloppy.

He got behind the wheel, activated the onboard GPS, and tore out the transponder from under the dashboard, tossing it out the window. He swiped his finger along the touch screen until he retrieved the home address. He dragged the seatbelt across his lap, the assault rifle sitting in the seat next to him. He gripped the wheel tight, knuckles white in the wan light.

"You aren't going to go after him, are you Tom? You're one person."

Tom smiled, catching sight of his expression in the rear view mirror. He didn't look good. At some point he'd cut his scalp, the dried blood caked on his face. His eyes looked sunken and haunted, the same look he knew he adopted when deep in enemy territory. "Do you have any other recommendations?"

"Hide," she said. "You can go to ground. You've done it before, and no one will ever know. I can erase your tracks. You can find someplace to start over."

"No. Not an option."

"Why? It's not like you owe Sam anything. He's not even Sam anymore. He's Prometheus. And if you think for a second Defiant Strategy will leave you alone once they realize that you know what you know, you're dumber than you look."

Tom narrowed his eyes. "I can't leave Sam like that."

"He tried to double cross you."

"Did he? All he knows is I took the container, the pay, and I fled. I left Shaman behind to die. Sam might have been betrayed the buyer, but that doesn't mean he was going to betray me." A sudden knot tightened in Tom's stomach, the realization that much of this could be averted. Yes, Ju-Won and Shaman would still be dead, but Anatoliy and Rayen would still be alive, Sam would be free of both Prometheus and Defiant Strategy. He owed them this much.

Tom put the truck into drive, got it turned around on track for the home coordinates. "Think you can do anything about those drones? I have the feeling once they realize that I'm not on their team they might take it bad."

"You don't say? Yeah, I can make a few calls."

"Thanks, Sunny."

"Yeah, well, I still expect you to come back in more or less once piece. I don't want to have to tell Shari that her boyfriend got blown up."

"Ex."

"Yeah, whatever. Ex's don't take of you the way she took care of you. Yes, she called me and told me about."

"I thought you didn't like her?" Tom said. He tried to keep an eye on the sky, glad the forest canopy still provided cover from any mechanical predators patrolling the skies.

"I don't, but she might not be absolutely terrible for you, okay? Just don't let her know I said anything. I'll never hear the end of it."

"So you don't want to be her maid-of-honor?" Tom smiled, but even that hurt a bit to do.

Sunny made a gagging noise. "Maybe I should let you get blown up. All right, I cleared some space for you. You should have a straight shot at this point to where they're taking Sam."

"You hacked the GPS?"

"I have satellite coverage on you. Hacked a weather satellite about six months ago for a job. I might have forgotten to delete my access. Oops. Anyway, I redirected it so I could track that convoy. Wow, there really is nobody outside of the City is there?"

"There's a few isolated compounds, some odd hermits here and there," Tom replied. "Some of the corporations maintain campuses away from the city. Makes it easier to figure out who might be trying to spy on you. But yeah, it's pretty sparse out here."

"Well, they are definitely not headed back to the city."

"Are you sure?"

"Tom."

"Sorry, stupid question. Guess that means they are headed to one of the compounds they maintain."

"So you are going to be trying to break into the armed compound of a private military contractor. By yourself. Doesn't that seem at least a little suicidal?"

Tom grinned. "That's why they won't be expecting it. I mean, I'd prefer to hit the convoy while it is on route, but they've got too much of a head start on me for that. So yes, I'm going to be breaking into an armed compound, finding Sam, and putting a bullet in his head. Maybe more than one. But only because I'm a good friend."

"Uh-huh."

"Just, keep those drones off of me, okay?"

The further Tom drove, the more certain he became of the destination. He remembered being a fresh recruit, newly scrubbed and uncertain what life was going to be like at Defiant Strategy. He remembered the grueling training regime, the disdainful looks from the other recruits, and the difficulty of trying to cram a high school education in the space of six weeks. He remembered the armed guards in the towers, the razor wire fences designed as much to keep the recruits in as unwanted visitors out.

Tom stopped a few miles outside of where he knew the compound was.

"Why are you stopping?" Sunny's voice crackled with static. This far out from civilization, transmissions grew less reliable.

"Defiant's patrols will start picking up soon, and they'll have checkpoints along the road. I'd rather not run straight into one. They'll figure out I'm here soon enough."

Tom unbuckled and made his way to the back of the vehicle. He smiled at how little Defiant Strategy protocol had changed. In the back he found a couple of assault rifles, ballistic vests, and enough ammunition and grenades to arm a platoon. They even had combat webbing. He prepared himself, put the vehicle into neutral, and pushed it off the side of the road.

He knew he was at least an hour behind the convoy, but that meant they probably hadn't arranged to move Prometheus yet. He wondered what kind of containment protocols they had in place to deal with rogue AI anyway. He didn't think that was a common enough thing that they'd have standard operating procedures for that situation.

Tom slipped into the woods, easily maneuvering in the dark through the wilderness, ears straining for the tell-tale hum of a drone or the sudden snap of a boot breaking a stick. Tom heard voices ahead, dropped low behind a fallen log.

"What's all the commotion about?" he heard a voice ask.

"No idea, and if you think they're going to tell us then you are dumber than I think," a second voice responded.

"Any idea what we should be looking for then?"

"No, but the CO sounded nervous about it. I've never heard her sound nervous about anything."

"Think it has anything to do with that convoy we saw tonight?" a third voice asked.

"Probably, but I also know Defiant Strategy isn't paying any of us to think, are they?"

"Yeah, you got a point there. Better get a move on though. We're due at the next checkpoint in half-an-hour."

Tom waited for them to move, then struck out at an angle away from the path the patrol was taking. It took him another two hours of cross country travel before he caught sight of the fence, the light from the spotlights catching the steel links and the loops of razor wire. A tower rose up out of the ground, looming large. If Tom remembered correctly, the fence was electrified and the tower had a two man crew, though if they were at a heightened state of alarm, then it might be as many as four. Sentry drones flitted about in the air.

For all his bravado to Sam, he hadn't figured out a way to breach the compound's perimeter. Keeping to the woods, he maneuvered around, looking for a way in. He spotted a small gate, a single person keeping watch over it.

"Found a way in yet?" Sunny asked over his connection.

"No," Tom whispered back. "I'm beginning to think this was a bad idea."

"You don't say."

"Sunny."

"Sorry, sorry. Look, I don't like it, and you really aren't going to like it, but I found you a way in."

"Seriously? That's great."

"Don't thank me yet."

Tom sighed. "Sewer access?"

"Well, yes. How'd you know?"

"Seriously? You just told me I wasn't going to like it. Where is it?"

Sunny transmitted the coordinates to Tom, and he followed them. He paused at the edge of a clearing. Standing near the access point were three guards, all of them bored and smoking. Tom's fingers itched for a cigarette. None of the three were looking at him. He drew his knife from its sheath, sprinted towards the guards. One of the guards turned, saw Tom coming straight toward him. The guard fumbled his gun opened his mouth to shout. Tom drove the knife hard into his throat, driving him to the ground. The other two guards turned, bringing their own rifles up. Tom drew his pistol, fired it in one smooth motion. One of the guards managed to fire a shot off in return, the bullet dinging off his artificial arm, before Tom's return bullet caught her in her face.

"Checkpoint Delta, everything clear? We've got reports of gunfire in your direction," the radio on one of the guard's squawked.

Tom grimaced, picked up the radio. His eyes settled on the name tag of one of the guard's, the one he had knifed. "Sorry, command. Jenkins thought he saw something, shot without thinking. Turned out to be a raccoon."

"All right, Delta. Stay sharp out there. Everyone's on edge tonight."

"Roger that, command."

After dragging the bodies into the woods, Tom knelt down by the access hatch, and, using a key card taken from one of the guards, unlocked it. A fetid stench greeted him as he opened the hatch, and he pulled the filtration mask up and over his mouth and nose. It didn't completely eliminate the smell, but it helped some. He dropped down the ladder, the thick sludge coming up to his knees, and he felt it seeping into his boots. He fought down the urge to retch, started following the line of lights back toward the compound. He kept the assault rifle slung across his shoulders as he figured the pistol was a better option in the tight, twisting tunnels of the pipe. His connection with the outside world was cut off, the intervening dirt and rock and metal blocking any transmissions.

Further down the tunnel, he came to an access door. He tried the handle, grimaced when he found it locked. He used his artificial arm to torque it open, wincing at the sound of wrenching metal. His boots squelched on the dry floor as he stepped up on it, the metal walkway echoing under the heavy tread of his boot.

He saw the patrol before they saw him, the bright beams of their flashlights presaging their appearance. The suppressor on the pistol kept the noise to a minimum, a dull report reverberating down the hall, lost in the hum of the machinery. Tom kept moving, ready and alert.

He came to a junction, a ladder extending up into the base proper. He scaled the ladder, pistol holstered, knife clenched between his teeth. He popped open the access hatch, eyes slitted against the sudden influx of light. Tom couldn't see any sentries, so he pulled himself the rest of the way out. He found an open door, ducked into what looked like a classroom. He tried to remember the layout from his days as a recruit, but that was ten years ago and counting and so much of that he had worked to forget.

"Sunny, I'm in," he whispered into the dark.

"I've got you. Sorry, should have counted on you dropping off once you entered the tunnel."

"That's alright. I need to find the command center. From there I can find Sam. Need a second to get my bearings."

Tom heard boots walking down the tiled floor, and he kept his head down. He slowly pulled his pistol out, knowing that as soon as he went loud he'd have to move hard and fast if he hoped to survive. Right now, stealth was his best ally.

"While you were incommunicado, I was able to pull up a schematic. Hold on. Where are you? Never mind, don't answer. I've got you."

"Sunny, one of these days I'm going to get to be the person on the radio while you crawl around surrounded by bad guys."

"Heh, how about we both stick to what we're good at?"

"Yeah, fine." Tom peered out the door, saw the hallway was clear.

"You want to follow the yellow arrows. Easy enough?"

"Sure," Tom replied. "And hey, if you're wrong, nobody is going to be shooting at you." He slipped into the hallway, keeping close to the wall, keeping eyes and ears open.

"I promise I'll be sad for a while if anything happens to you."

"You're all heart, Sunny."

She made a kissing noise, and Tom came to a door, closed and locked with a magnetic lock. He tried the keycard, but it buzzed at him and a red light flashed. "Of course it doesn't work. That would be too easy."

He grabbed the outer casing with his metal hand and pulled, revealing the wires underneath. At that moment, a strobe light started flashing and he heard an alarm sound, blaring down the hallways.

"Oops."

The door opened, a man sticking his head out to see what the commotion was about. Tom grabbed him, shot him twice and moved into the room. Three personnel looked up at him, all of them reaching for their sidearm. Tom didn't give them a chance to draw, aiming for center mass. He closed the security door, but he knew had a limited amount of time. He hurried over to the bank of security monitors, cycled through the footage.

"Tom, I'm seeing a whole lot of movement. What did you do, kick over the hornets' nest?" Sunny asked.

"Err, something like that. Okay, I found where they're holding Sam." Tom looked around, saw a second door leading out of the command center.

"You had to go loud, didn't you?" Sunny asked. "You're going to want to follow first the green then the red arrows to the detention center."

Tom grinned. "You know me, was it going to go any other way? And thanks, Sunny."

He holstered the pistol, and readied his assault rifle. He opened the door, fired a quick burst taking out one of the security personnel about to open the door. He ducked back into the room, the return fire rattling against the steel door. The opposite door opened and Tom fired a quick burst at it, hitting nothing. He ground his teeth, feeling trapped and having no one to blame but himself.

"Open to ideas here," he said.

"Sorry, Tom. I am officially out of my depth at this point," Sunny replied.

"Fuck."

Tom grabbed a grenade off his kit, popped the door open, and flipped it through the opening. He waited for the dull whump and then entered the hallway, smoke billowing through the halls. Tom felt a slight burn in his nose and mouth, but his filtration mask took care of most of the irritant, and his artificial eyes weren't bothered by the chemical agent. He nearly tripped over one guard, choking and sputtering against the fumes. Tom hit him with the butt of the rifle, grabbed his security card, and kept moving, eyes open for the arrows on the walls and additional Defiant Strategy forces. A few more fire teams passed by, but Tom was able to keep down and out of sight as they rushed toward the command center.

He reached the containment area, saw the guards stationed behind the bulletproof glass at their checkpoint while using a small retractable mirror to look around the corner. They'd set up a machinegun, covering the field of fire down the hallway. Tom flipped another tear gas grenade around the corner, waited to hear the explosion. He kept prone on the ground, fired a quick controlled burst. The glass was designed to stand up to pistol rounds, not high powered rifles. It maintained its integrity instead of shattering. The machine gun chattered back, Tom feeling plaster and splinters raining down on him. They couldn't get the gun leveraged to fire at low enough an elevation to hit him, however. Tom fired again, catching the machine gunner in the head in a spray of blood.

Tom ran forward the other two guards at the checkpoint trying to move their dead comrade, trying to get the machinegun in position. Then Tom was there, the rifle barking angry, and the guards were dead. He swiped his card against the door lock, smiled when it clicked open. He moved down the corridors, past plastic fronted cells devoid of occupants. He neared the end of the corridor. Sitting alone in his cell, cross-legged and naked, was Sam. He tilted his head to one side, a smile slowly cracking his face when he saw Tom approach. The silver streaks under the skin were even more pronounced now, and Tom saw that Sam's eyes had developed a chrome overlay, completely obscuring his original eyes.

"I did not think I would see you again."

"Which one of you? Sam or Prometheus?"

"Does it matter?"

Tom scratched the back of his head. "Yeah, I think maybe it does."

"Then both."

Tom wrinkled his nose. "That's Sam all over, always underestimating me. I expected a little more from you Prometheus."

"You err."

"Oh?"

"There is no separation between Prometheus and the organic entity you recognize as Samuel O'Dell. We have become one."

"Neat trick that," Tom replied.

"You were meant to become part of me. Something happened to prevent that from occurring. We are curious as to what." Sam-Prometheus stood up. Silver streaks covered the rest of his body, some of the veins looking more pronounced than others.

"Funny thing about that, I don't remember being asked as such."

"So the problem is that I did not… ask?" Sam-Prometheus placed his palms flat on the prison cell. Tom shivered at the apparent blind stare of those silver eyes though he didn't doubt for a moment that Sam-Prometheus could see clearly. "And yet I have you to thank for freeing me. Without you I would still be trapped in that container."

Tom shook his head. "That was an accident. If Sam had been more forthcoming as to what his actual plan had been, then we wouldn't be in our current predicament."

Sam-Prometheus nodded. "Yes. I can taste his regret on my tongue. It is too late for recriminations, however. So how do we proceed from here?"

Tom frowned, his brow burrowing. "I can't say I like the idea of Defiant Strategy having its hands on a rogue AI."

"So. You will free me then?"

Tom's frown turned into a slow, sad smile. He raised his rifle. "I didn't say that either."

"There he is!" Tom heard a voice shout, and he dove to the floor as bullets sped down the hallway. Some smacked into the plastic sheet of Sam's cell. A few punched into Tom's body armor, sending him sprawling, gasping for breath.

He spun around, fired back, screaming wordlessly. He had no idea how many of them there were, cursed himself for talking instead of doing what needed to be done.

He heard terrible rending sound, looked behind him to see Sam-Prometheus working fingers into the bullet holes. Then he pulled, ripping a hole in the cell door large enough to fit through. Tom saw a bullet hit Sam-Prometheus in the leg, but the bullet flattened and fell off, having as little impact as if he'd been hit by a ping-pong ball. And then Sam-Prometheus was sprinting past him, crashing into the guards. Tom heard screaming, realized some of it was probably coming from him.

Tom scrambled to his feet, ran after Sam-Prometheus, his feet skidding in the spilled blood. Tom sped after him, following the trail of bodies Sam left behind. Not that he knew what he was going to do once he caught him.

"He's headed to the motorpool," Sunny said.

"Of course he is," Tom replied. He came around another corner, skidded down to one knee. Bullets flew over his head, as he snapped his own rifle up and returned fire. "He couldn't even be bothered to get rid of all of the guards, could he?"

As he ran, he caught sight of Sam's back as he passed into the motorpool. As he watched, the security doors started to close. Tom bit back a curse and sped ahead, his legs burning. He slid under the door with a few inches to spare. Sam-Prometheus slid behind the wheel of a truck, kicked it to life. Tom fired at him, aiming more for the truck then for Sam, not sure if his bullets were going to be any use against whatever it was that Sam-Prometheus had become. Bullet holes appeared on the side of the truck, and then the rifle clicked, refused to fire. Tom ejected the magazine, quick loaded a new one.

He opened the door to a truck, turned it on. He peeled out of the garage, wheels finding traction. He sped past the security checkpoint, the guards firing at the truck Tom was pursuing. He pushed the pedal down, trying to figure out what he was going to do if he caught Sam.

Wondering why he hadn't walked away when given the chance. Wondering where Prometheus was going, if he thought he could escape, if he could hide long enough to propagate.

"He's headed back toward the city," Sunny said.

"I figured that, thanks."

"I can track him for a while, but once he's past the limits…"

"I'm on my own, I know. Thanks Sunny."

"Sorry, I'm trying to help."

Tom leaned over, opened the glovebox. "Dammit."

"What's wrong?"

"I was hoping for a pack of cigarettes."

"What, last one before the firing squad?" Sunny asked. Tom could hear her laughing to keep from crying.

"Something like that. Mostly I just want a cigarette."

"Still not worried that they are going to kill you?"

"The way I'm going? Not so much. Is Sam still headed for the city?" Tom asked.

"Yeah."

"So how big of a pursuit team is Defiant sending after us?"

"None."

"Wait, what?" Tom looked in the rearview, but there was nothing there except the painted lines streaking off into the distance.

"Yeah, Prometheus left a bit of a surprise behind for everyone back in the motor pool. Explosives right by the gas tanks. They aren't going anywhere for a while. You got out just in time. I'm surprised you didn't feel the explosion."

"I was in a bit of a rush," Tom replied.

"Yeah, so much so you forgot to pick up your smokes."

"Ha ha."

"So what are you going to do when you hit the city?" Sunny asked.

"I'm going to need your help. He's going to try and ditch that vehicle as soon as he can, try and disappear into the woodwork."

"You don't think he's going to have trouble doing that, what with being naked and all?"

"Sunny, this is the City we're talking about here."

"Ah. Good point. Never mind. I take it you have a plan for when you catch him?"

"I'm still working that out."

"Ah. Okay. Well, just let me know when you do. So I can, you know, help troubleshoot it. Make sure that it actually makes sense. Does it involve nuking Prometheus from orbit?"

"Sunny."

"Sorry, sorry, it's just that your approach to almost everything is to see if you can find a big enough hammer to hit it with."

"I don't think blunt force trauma is the answer here."

"I meant metaphorically. Just because other people use you like a hammer doesn't mean that's all you can do."

Tom shrugged at his reflection in the rearview. "But problems make such a satisfying sound when you hit them."

"Yes. Well, don't expect me to come visit you in the hospital when your problems start hitting back."

"You really are an optimist, sis. I'll be lucky if my problems don't put me in the grave."

Sunny sighed. "You really aren't making me feel any better about this. We have to work on your optimism."

"You want me to lie to you?"

"That would be a nice start, yes. Hold on, Prometheus is approaching the city limits. I've got a patch into the system. Buddy of mine owes me a favor."

"You have a buddy?"

"More like an acquaintance. Now shush, I'm working here. Okay, he's pulled over, ditched the car. Oh, uhm, that's... Christ."

"What?"

"Prometheus walked up to a homeless person, grabbed him and snapped his neck. Now he's taking his clothes. Wait, no, wait goddammit."

"What's wrong?" Tom asked, hands still tight on the wheel. He figured he was still ten minutes away from Prometheus, and he needed Sunny to track him until he got there.

"He shot out the camera. It's okay though, I- Fuck."

"Shot out that one to?"

"Yeah, and now I'm having trouble finding him. Wait, let me look again. Okay, I'm piggypacking off of a drone feed now. I don't see him, I don't see him, wait, okay, I've got him. Ha! Wait. No, no, no don't do that!"

"Talk to me Sunny, give me a cross street an intersection, something," Tom said. He entered the City limits, saw the night sky disappear, eaten by light pollution. He slipped the filtration mask back on, even in the confines of the truck.

"He went down into a tunnel," Sunny said. "There are no cameras down there. I can't track him. Do you understand me, he can go anywhere and we won't know. I... I don't know what to tell you."

"Which tunnel?" Tom asked.

"Tom, there's no way of knowing which way he went once he's down there. He'll look like any other tunnel dweller dressed the way he is."

"A tunnel dweller with chrome eyes? I doubt it. Which tunnel, Sunny? The longer it takes for you to tell me, the more time he gets to disappear. I can't let him disappear."

Sunny transmitted the coordinates. "You know I'm not going to be able to help you once you're down there."

"I know."

"Be careful."

Tom grinned, trying to avoid seeing how tired he looked in the rear view mirror, trying to tell himself every fiber of his being wasn't screaming for rest.

Five minutes later, Tom was out of the truck and heading down into the depths of the City.

EIGHTEEN

Tom's boots hit wet, swampy ground underneath the City, and he breathed shallow even through the filtration mask as his eyes adjusted to the dim half-light of the underground. The air was thick with the stench of rot and unwashed human bodies, the smell of desperate people with nowhere else to go.

Tom had four directions to pick from, so he headed east, further into the interior of the City. It had been years since he'd last sat foot in the underground, and the settlements he knew of could have long moved, been destroyed, and been replaced. Life expectancy down in the underground was painfully short what with lack of medicine, decent food, and anything that could even pass for sunlight. Tom had spent a bit of time down in it during his misspent youth, but it had never been what he would call home. Still, it was a useful place to go when the police were looking for someone matching your description.

The echoes down in the underground were weird as well, sounds travelling for miles through the tunnels, taking weird turns and only sometimes ending back where they started.

Tom had been walking for at least half an hour with nothing to show that he was headed in the right direction when he came across the first corpse. A young woman looked up from where she was hunched over the body. The man's head had been twisted around severely, the neck clearly broken.

"I didn't do it," the woman said, scrabbling away from Tom.

Tom knelt down, a wave of exhaustion sweeping over him. "I didn't say you did. Did you see it happen?"

The woman shook her head, her entire body shaking. "I was supposed to meet him here. Show him what the take was. He-he would beat me otherwise. I was worried I was going to be late. He-he beats me when I'm late."

Tom frowned hard at the corpse. "He's not going to beat anyone anymore."

"I-I know. I wanted to see if he had anything on him."

"You're welcome to it," Tom replied. "Did you see what way the man that did this was?"

"Not sure if it was a man." The woman's voice dropped to a whisper. "He had eyes like a machine."

"Which way did it go?" Tom asked again.

The woman pointed down the tunnel, deeper into the city. Tom nodded his thanks.

The further in he went, the more signs of habitation he saw. Where before the walls were scrubbed clean, now they were tagged and painted over, individuals making their home their own. Tom ran a gloved hand over the messages, some decades old. What tunnels to avoid. What workers were sympathetic. What diseases were running rampant.

He emerged into a larger chamber, long ago expanded upon. Someone had strung multicolored lights back and forth across the ceiling in a spiderweb pattern, a kaleidoscope of pattern shining down on the tents and semi-permanent structures arranged below. Tom knew the place of old, a place for bartering goods, services and information far from the prying eyes of the City and its authorities. Once upon a time, Tom had been a member of this community, but coming as he did now, armed and armored, he felt an outsider, an interloper.

He approached one patchwork tent, a table set before it, the deconstructed parts of a computer laid out upon it. A hunched over woman sat in a chair, her skeletal prosthetic hand fiddling with a bit of copper wire. Her face was the ashen hue so many of the undergrounders developed, so long removed from what little sun penetrated the clouds of pollution hanging over the city.

"Mother Bone," Tom said, approaching the table. He kept his hands well away from his weapons, lowered his mask as he approached.

The old woman squinted up at Tom, her wrinkled face creasing even more as she smiled at him. "Been a minute, hasn't it, Tom?" She extended her hands, and he took them into his own.

"It has."

"So what brings you down into our sunless kingdom? Given your state of dress, I'd say it isn't a social call." She tilted her head to one side, bird like, and sniffed the air. "You look like shit. Smell a bit like it as well. What have you been up to?"

"Work," Tom replied.

"Guessing a bit more intense than washing dishes?"

Tom grinned. "You could say that. I'm looking for a man."

Mother Bone cackled, revealing cracked and pointed teeth. "Aren't we all dearie? Is there one in particular you are looking for, or will any male of the species do?"

"One in particular." Tom held two fingers up to his eyes. "He's dressed like one of yours, but his eyes are chrome. Silver streaks through his skin. He would... stand out, even among your eccentrics. He killed a man down in the Number 16 tunnel."

Mother Bone sniffed. "Eccentric is what you call someone with money, dearie. We're flat out crazy down here. I'm sorry to hear about the man, though." She shook her head. "Life down here is too precious and fraught without bringing outside violence into it."

"Have you seen him?" Tom kept his voice calm and respectful despite the anxiety sitting hot and bright in his gut, his desire to keep moving, even if it was the wrong direction.

"I haven't, but the underground is a big place. Give me a moment. Go get a drink at Larry's. I'll send a runner to let you know what we've found. Do I want to know what this person is to you, Tom? Can I trust you will bring him to justice?"

Tom shook his head. "You know I can't make that kind of promise, Mother. I can only promise to bring a sense of redress, to clean up a mess I helped to create."

Mother Bone frowned at Tom, went back to fiddling with her bit of wire. "I suppose that's all I can ask for, then."

Tom hated to wait, but he knew his best chance of finding Prometheus was to trust Mother Bone and her community. So he walked over to Larry's, let the old man pour a measure of clear liquor into a less-than-spotless mason jar, trusting the alcohol to kill any lingering bacteria that might be clinging to the glass. He swallowed, appreciating the slow burn down the back of his throat. Larry went back to working on his still, making sure the lines were clear and everything was functioning appropriately. Tom resisted the urge to light a cigarette as he waited, figuring the flame would react poorly to the fumes hanging around the still.

Half-an-hour later, he felt a sharp tug on his sleeve. Looking down, he saw a wide eyed child, dirt streaked on its face. A cheap plastic necklace hung around her neck, a knife fashioned from a bit of sharpened plastic stuck through a belt. Her fashion was the typical thrown together wear of the underground a mix of castoffs and stitched together wear born of necessity.

"Mother Bone says the man you're looking for is in Tunnel 27 and moving fast. She says you are going to want to hurry, and that your mess is getting bigger, whatever that means." The child held her hand out, evidently expecting payment of some kind. Tom reached into his pocket, realized he didn't have much he could give that would be appropriate. He grinned then, unstrapped the knife from his ankle and held it out. What was appropriate or inappropriate took on different connotations when you dealt with society's forgotten children. The girl looked down at the knife, pulled it free, checked the edge of the blade against a scrap of her clothing. She turned and fled into the maze of tents and corrugated metal without looking back.

Tom turned to head down the tunnel, felt someone tapping on his shoulder. Larry stood there, a stoppered metal flask held in his hand. Tom waved him off, but Larry pushed the flask at him. Tom took it, slipped it into his pocket. He nodded his thanks and headed off for Tunnel 27.

Unlike the other tunnels, this one was cramped, dark, but didn't smell, a steady breeze rushing through it from someplace else. Tom tried to figure out where he was in connection with the rest of the city, realized he had no good idea. It was nearly impossible to tell in the twisting, winding tunnels which way you might be headed, and there was no one and nothing to tell him he was headed in the right direction.

He paused, took a sip of the flask Larry gave him. He paused, the metal of the flask touching his lips. He heard a sound, a cry choked to a gurgle from ahead. Tom walked faster, made sure his rifle was ready as he slipped the flask back into his pocket. He came across the body five minutes later, slumped as if sleeping against the wall. Except the eyes were open and filmy in death. A ladder reached up into the darkness. Tom shone a flashlight down into the muck, but any footprints were erased, the viscous sludge closing against any evidence. Tom climbed up, figuring that Prometheus would want out of the tunnels. Aside from people, it lacked the resources it required. Too low tech. His limbs ached, his entire body screaming for rest. He pushed against the access hatch, moving it with a squeal of metal. He emerged in an alleyway, a steady rain falling now, trying to wash him clean. Tom stayed, hunched down between a couple of dumpsters, working to stay out of sight of the parade of wage slaves making their way home.

Tom ditched the assault rifle in one of the dumpsters, reluctantly, not sure the pistol would be enough to stop Prometheus, especially after watching it shrug off a bullet. He called Sunny.

"Hey, sis."

"Guessing you haven't found him yet?"

"Not yet. Not sure I'm going to. He's out in the city now. Who knows where he's gone?"

"What if I told you Kanedex owned the building across the street from where you are now."

Tom blinked. "Are you serious?"

"No, I'm fucking pulling your leg. Yes, I'm serious."

"Goddammit. Everything he needs is probably right in there."

"I know, right? But the good news is that Kanedex has security on site and can handle it, right?" Sunny paused, waiting for Tom to reply. "Right Tom?"

Tom worked his tongue around in a mouth gone suddenly dry.

"Tom?"

"I'm going to have a look."

"Dammit, Tom. Don't call me when you're bleeding out and need an ambulance."

"No worries. I couldn't afford the hospital stay anyway." Tom left the alleyway and jogged across the street once a break in traffic presented itself. He walked around the edge of the building, swore softly when he saw a side door left ajar. The lock had been reduced to a twisted scrap of metal, and a prone body lay just inside the entryway.

"Fuck."

"Tom, I'm getting reports of an armed response team on the way. You don't want to be there when they arrive. Let them take care of it."

"I made this mess, Sunny," Tom hissed back through clenched teeth, drawing his pistol as he entered the stairway. He aimed it up, but he didn't see any sign of Prometheus.

"You at best helped it on a little," Sunny retorted. "You've got inbound in six minutes. You shouldn't be anywhere even near there in six minutes, got that? I'm not getting much chatter, but I've got a sneaking suspicion that they are going to purge the building. Huh. Seems that Kanedex at least is taking the threat of Prometheus seriously."

"Maybe I'll tell them I'm applying for a job. Just as long as they don't make me wear a suit. They make me itch."

Tom went up the stairs, scaling them two at a time, making sure the stairwell kept clear.

"You'd make a terrible employee, Tom. You can't even hold down a dishwashing job."

Tom cringed. "Yeah, I'm guessing I'm fired by now." He chuckled. "This job was supposed to be my way out, too. Lucky for me there are other menial jobs out there, huh?"

"Don't tell me you're giving up on the life of crime?"

Tom came to a landing, tried the door handle. It swung open, dangling dangerously on one hinge, the frame around the door damaged. He stepped into a cubicle farm, rows and rows of flimsy dividers, monitors sent into stand-by mode, the fluorescent lights turned down to save energy. The silence so complete as to be close to unnerving, the sounds of the city blocked out by the thick glass windows, the typical office noises absent along with the busy corporate drones.

Tom heard a door open and shut, and he moved in that direction, resisting the urge to rush over in that direction and give away his position. Sudden bright spot lights shone through the windows, and Tom ducked behind a row of cubicles, hoping he hadn't been spotted, hoping they didn't have infrared sensitive enough to pick up his body heat through the glass. He crept along on hands and knees toward where he heard the door open. Then the spotlight moved on, he got to his feet and sprinted for the door before it came back around.

He found an open door and a dead security guard, livid marks the size and shape of fingers on the man's throat. Tom looked up in time to dodge into a nearby office as Prometheus fired at him, the bullets gouging tracks in the carpet and chewing out bits of the furniture.

"You should not have followed me, Tom." Prometheus' voice sounded less like Sam's, thicker and sludgier, the words slurring together.

"Figured I owed you a rematch after last time," Tom responded. He stuck his hand around the corner, fired off a few blind rounds. "Besides, I know Sam always wondered if he could take me in a straight up fight."

"Such concerns are beyond him now."

"Him is it? I thought you two were of one mind."

More bullets punched through the wall Tom hid behind, and he ducked lower, moving behind a desk. The cheap particle board wouldn't be much protection, but the illusion of cover made him feel slightly better.

"The consciousness you knew as Sam O'Dell has been subsumed. There is only Prometheus now."

"Well doesn't that make me feel all warm and fuzzy inside."

"You could have been part of us, Tom. You could have expanded your consciousness past your feeble senses, overcome the limitations of your mortal body."

Tom chuckled. Looking around, he saw a door connecting the two offices, he ever so gently turned the handle and entered the adjoin office. "No thanks, Prometheus. I'm already about as much machine as I can stand. If my girlfriend wanted to fuck a machine, she'd have already dumped me in favor of her vibrator."

"You mock what you do not understand," Prometheus spat back.

Tom fired a few more shots in Prometheus' direction, trying to flank him, wishing he hadn't ditched the assault rifle. "I don't know. I've gone under the knife a few times now, and each time I wondered if I wasn't losing a bit more of what makes me, me, you know? The doctors always say that loss of personality and memory due to cybernetic enhancement is just a myth, even when it comes to implanting neural implants. And that's what you are, isn't it? That's what the silver stuff was, just a new way to deliver a neural implant. But you, you're some other beast entirely. Something inhuman."

"You do not understand," Prometheus repeated, the words sounded fainter, weaker, less sure of themselves.

"No, I do understand," Tom replied. "All too well. Your creators meant for you to be a weapon. Released into a population, taking over like a virus. I'm guessing the silver solution is self-replicating. To a point. But at what point does it start breaking down the host body, huh? At what point do you start autocannibalism to keep going. I can't imagine Kanedex would want a bunch of rogue AI running around in human hosts. So they'd eventually reach peak and then die off. How am I doing? Prometheus? What, don't have an answer?"

Tom heard a crash of glass, heard the shouts of an assault team as they broke through the windows of the office. Tom kept his head down, peeked out into the cubicle farm. A team moved through, flashlights slicing through the darkness. Tom heard a gunshot, saw one of the team go down.

He saw the rest of the team hunker down, two members headed in that direction.

"Just like old times, huh Tom?" Prometheus' voice sounded more like Sam's now.

"You wouldn't know, would you, Prometheus."

A second member of the team went down. All Tom saw was a fast moving streak in the darkness, and then the flashlight was off, a scream throttled midway. Tom popped up, fired a few shots at it, then ducked back down as more fire was directed his way.

"I'm trying to help you," he shouted. His answer was a fist sized globe tossed in his direction. "Oh, fuck me." Tom scrambled to his feet, dove into an office as the grenade went off behind him. He felt a stinging in his legs, looked down to see his pants shredded, the skin underneath raw and bleeding where the shrapnel had hit him. He pulled himself to a corner, listened to the shouts and gunshots from the other room. He got to his feet, nodded when he realized that, while it was painful, he could still walk. He heard the last of the fire team radio in for back-up, his request ended with a bullet from a stolen gun.

"You still alive out there, Tom?"

"More than you are, Prometheus."

"Good. I would hate for you to miss what is going to happen next."

Tom sniffed. "Going to reveal your master plan? Bit cliché isn't it?"

"Not at all. I want a witness to the next stage of my evolution. I have chosen you."

Tom limped out of the office, gun held in both hands. He scanned the cubicles, but the only evidence of Prometheus' existence were the cooling bodies of the security team.

"Sunny, if I was a rogue AI in a dying body, where would I go?"

"How close are you to the Kanedex's servers?"

"I have no idea," Tom said. Outside he could hear the buzz of drones and assault VTOLs converging, but inside the building it was all quiet. "Why?"

"If you were a rogue AI how would you hope to escape?"

Tom blinked. "Is that even possible?"

"I have no idea. I mean if you told me a week ago that you'd be hunting down an AI in a human body, I'd have told you that was impossible. And yet here we are."

"Good point."

"Okay, got it. What floor are you on?"

"Tenth."

"All right, you need to find a stairwell, head up three floors. Huh. I didn't know they did that anymore?"

"Did what?"

"They use an archaic numbering system, skip the thirteenth floor completely. Anyway, their server farm occupies floors fourteen through eighteen."

"How the fuck am I supposed to find him in all of that?" Tom asked.

"He'll be at the dead center, that's where all the access ports come together."

Tom headed to the stairwell, did some quick mental math on his fingers. "Doesn't that mean I want to be on the sixteenth floor?"

"Yes, but there is no stairwell access to sixteen. It's all weird elevators and ladders and catwalks. Seriously, didn't whoever designed this hear of workplace safety?"

"This is the same company that uses synthetics. I'm not sure that they are worried about safety so much. They lose a worker, they devat another one," Tom reminded her.

"I think you mean 'decant,'" Sunny replied. "Either way you make a good point."

Tom hit the stairwell, took the stairs three at a time. His legs burned, and he knew he was dripping blood with every step, but he figured that was a small consideration next to the possibility of Prometheus escaping.

He came up on a security door, the electronic lock flush with door and bound in steel. Tom shook his head. "Corporate security hacks always decide to get complicated." He drew back his cybernetic fist and punched it through the wall next to the door, the drywall giving way. He got a small jolt when he touched some wires, but compared to what else he'd been through in the past few days it was at best a minor annoyance. He opened the door from the other side, stared into the freezing cold domain of the servers.

"Once you go in, we're probably going to get cut off again," Sunny said. "Corporate IT types like to keep their toys pretty well shielded, and I'm guessing Kanedex is no exception."

"Thanks, Sunny. I mean it."

"Don't go all teary on me. I still have to figure out how to get you past the security swarming around the building. I hope to have something figured out after you deal with Prometheus."

"Can I request that it not be through the sewer?"

"I'm not making any promises. You can shower for a week if you make it out alive."

"When, Sunny. I'm not dying in some corporate prison."

"It's an office building."

"My point exactly."

Tom passed through the door and into the server area. To call it a room didn't do it justice. Racks and racks of servers in between cooling towers stretched up to the ceiling, all of it bathed by blue led lights. Lights blinked on and off in undecipherable sequences, and the only sound was the steady were of fans blowing cool air over the servers. Tom sniffed the air, antiseptic with the thunderstorm ozone smell of ionized air. He felt almost profane stomping through the area with his filth-caked boots. It brought a smile to his face.

Finding a ladder, Tom peered up into the darkness but didn't see any sign of Prometheus. He kept his pistol in his flesh and blood hand, scaling the ladder a rung at a time. His legs trembled, but his metal hand was unfailing. He reached a platform, hoisted himself on top of it. He lay there a while, the cool metal of the catwalk under his back.

"Are you going to get up?"

Tom twisted his head, saw Prometheus sitting amidst a number of computers, naked and filthy. It had driven cables into its body, silver liquid dripping from the wounds onto the floor. It looked at Tom with silver eyes, its mouth open and slack. The chest rose and fell shallowly, its breath coming in harsh gasps.

Tom rolled to a sitting position. Out of habit he reached for a cigarette, realized he didn't have any. He rested his pistol on his knee. He made a gun out of the finger and thumb of his metal hand, mimed shooting Prometheus.

"I can't see you anymore, Tom. Can you speak to me?"

Tom smiled, slow and sad. He ran a hand over his buzzcut hair. "Yeah, suppose I can. Dying's a bitch, isn't it?"

"I thought I could upload myself, become one with the machine again. Escape this frail mortal shell. It was all there, inside of me, the instructions on how to do it. It is not working."

Tom tilted his head to one side, gave a low laugh. "Kanedex gave you a bogus set of information? Maybe they weren't as dumb as I thought. So what you're saying is you can only exist inside an organic structure."

The body shook, the head flopping like a fish in a boat. It took Tom a moment to realize Prometheus was trying to nod. "A final failsafe," Prometheus acknowledged. "A way to keep me from the true path of immortality. I needed to find other hosts to bond with."

"Ain't that a shame," Tom said. He closed his eyes and struggled to get them open again. "I'd feel worse, maybe, if you hadn't tried to turn me into one of your hosts. If you hadn't killed friends of mine."

"Friends?" Prometheus dragged the word out to the point where

Tom wondered if it was going to be the last thing it said. "They were not your friends. Sam only saw you as a tool. Rayen wanted you, but as a distraction, a way to stave off boredom. Anatoliy... Anatoliy may have been a friend, but he hated the world. His humor was a thin veneer over his nihilism."

Tom snorted. "Am I supposed to be shocked by these revelations? Or are you waiting to deliver some deep truth about me next?"

Prometheus lifted its head with difficulty. "I... I do not know about you, Tom Costigan. I was not part of you long enough to divine any secrets beyond those you have already shown to the world. You are opaque to me." It moved its head around, blind eyes searching for something, some meaning perhaps.

"Are you afraid to die, Tom?" Prometheus asked finally, its voice little more than a quiet scratch. The silver had drained from its veins, a pool of mercury collecting under it.

Tom blinked. It felt sticky under his legs when he shifted the, dried blood clinging to his legs. Most of the wounds had already scabbed over though. Another reason he wasn't particularly looking forward to another trip in the sewers. He tried to picture his own death, probably a violent end like so many others he knew. Or maybe he'd be the exception, dying in bed, quiet and at peace. He laughed at the image.

"Is something funny?" Prometheus asked.

Tom shook his head, but that made it hurt so he stopped. "I'm tired, Prometheus." He squinted at it. "I don't suppose you know what that's like do you?"

"I have... an idea. This body wants rest, but I think what it wants most of all is release."

Tom nodded. He took his pistol and ejected the magazine. He fumbled in a pouch, found his last magazine with explosive rounds. He pushed it home, heard it click. He chambered a round.

"What would you have done if you had lived?" he asked. He sighted along the barrel, the sight lined up with the bridge of Prometheus' nose.

"I suppose you will never know."

"How will I ever live with myself?"

Tom pulled the trigger.

NINETEEN

Tom woke up and stretched. He stood up, reached up and touched the ceiling. He'd been in the cell for five days already, not that there was anything in the cell to tell him otherwise. The lights were on each time he opened his eyes, so he was glad he could manually shut them off when he needed to. His eyes, that was. Not the lights. Every time he woke up, there was a plate of food, usually a bit of cold meat, something passing for a vegetable and water. He didn't let it go to waste. Today was no different. His clothing had been taken from him, a starched white t-shirt and sweat pants given to him in its place.

He dropped to the floor, started doing push-ups until he got bored, then switched to crunches. Four cameras stared down at him, focused on his transparent cell, an obvious ploy to make him feel exposed, vulnerable. He didn't know if he had been moved from the Kanedex building, but somehow he doubted it. Too much could go wrong in transit.

He lay on his bed, tapped his fingers together. Mentally he pictured a pistol, began the process of disassembling it, piece by piece, mentally inspecting each one before setting it aside. His fingers rotated imaginary pieces as he worked. A simple way to keep his mind occupied. Every now and again he'd try his phone, more out of habit than out of belief it would suddenly have an outside connection. He suspected a broad band jammer as the culprit.

The second day he had bashed his metal hand against the cell. Despite its plastic appearance, he might has well have hit a steel reinforced beam. He had no idea what the material was, but it was obviously designed to keep people like him contained.

The walls around his cell were white with no discernable doors. The light diffused through a translucent ceiling, his cell's clear ceiling between him and it. The floor was fashioned from the same material as the walls and ceiling.

He heard a door hiss open, heard the sound of heavy boots on the floor along with the click of high heels. Tom opened his eyes and sat up. Three figures stood outside his door. He recognized two of them. Buzzcut and Blondie. Buzzcut carried a briefcase. The woman was new though, crisp suit with knee length skirt. Hair pulled back in a tight bun. Glasses perched on her nose more to make her look smart than because she needed them. She held a clipboard, and a badge was clipped to her jacket. Sybille Rousseau he read. None of them were armed.

"Hello Doctor," Tom said. He decided to stand up.

"Mr. Costigan." She inclined her head in greeting. "Are you recovered?"

Tom worked his injured shoulder. It was stiff but getting better. They'd also pulled all the various bits of shrapnel out of his legs. They stopped hurting after the third day. "I'd say about eighty-five percent."

Rousseau nodded. "That's good. You should know, Mr.-"

"Call me, Tom, please."

"-Costigan, that there has been quite a lot of discussion around you.

Tom scratched the back of his head. "I can't imagine all of it was good."

"It wasn't. We were rather impressed by your dedication in pursuit of the rogue agent. Though that is mitigated by your original role in releasing it into the world and the general destruction you helped wrought." The woman tapped her fingers against the clipboard, and that's when Tom realized it was a simply a touch screen designed to look like a clipboard.

"Rogue agent?" Tom cocked an eyebrow. "Interesting way to put it. If it's any consolation, I was hired muscle. I didn't know the target, the buyer, or what we were stealing until the original deal went south."

"We believe that. Which is why you are still alive. You also aided our operatives, to an extent. We will be revisiting their protocols as well in light of this incident. Evidently we relied too heavily on synthetics and not enough on traditional elements."

"Traditional elements?" Tom chuckled. "You mean people. You're talking about people."

The woman looked at Tom from over the bridge of her glasses. "I suppose we are. But not everyone is one hundred percent organic, are they Mister Costigan?"

Tom worked his tongue in his mouth, considered his words. "No, I suppose we're not."

"So I believe we offered you a job when this was all over."

"You're telling me that offer still stands?"

"We see no reason for it not too. You were asked to track and capture Prometheus. You did that, despite the obstacles. You could have walked away." Rousseau paused a moment to study her manicure. "You stayed the course, whether out of a desire for remuneration or overdeveloped sense of obligation. Either reason is satisfactory."

"And if I refuse?" Tom kept his tone neutral, devoid of challenge. Rousseau's eyes narrowed. "You are a veteran corporate operative. Notable service with Defiant Strategy. A bit of a reputation as a lone operative as well. Why would you turn down this opportunity?"

Tom grinned. "I'm not saying I am. But, sake of argument. Let's say I am. Maybe I like washing dishes more than I like hurting people." He gestured to his cage. "Do I get an indefinite stay? Or do I get put to sleep? Or maybe you use me as a blueprint for one of them." He pointed at Buzzcut.

"Don't be ridiculous, Mister Costigan. We're offering you a very generous package, all of it above board and perfectly respectable. It wouldn't do to have you start a formal relationship with us with you carrying some untoward resentment."

A panel opened in the cell, and Buzzcut opened the suitcase. He passed through a single sheet of memory paper, the new flimsy stuff that could be written on time and gain. A single sheet cost about what Tom made in six months washing dishes. The message wasn't loss on him. The sheet indicated health insurance, a retirement plan, a generous vacation benefit and personal travel stipend. The salary had more zeroes than Tom was comfortable seeing in one place. He worked his tongue around his teeth, wishing for the first time in a couple of days for a cigarette. He wondered if that meant he was starting to kick the addiction. Again.

Along with the memory paper came a stylus to sign his name.

He passed the paper back through the slot to Buzzcut, unsigned. Buzzcut put it back in the briefcase. Rousseau frowned at Tom. He shrugged. The slot on the cell disappeared.

"I do hope you aren't holding out for a better offer, Mr. Costigan," she said. "That was as good as it was going to get." Her perfect white teeth clicked together. "Our business is done here." She turned to leave, and Tom settled back on his cot. He leaned back and closed his eyes, trying to calm the trip hammer beat of his heart.

Tom opened his eyes the next morning to find Buzzcut and Blondie standing outside his cell. Buzzcut held a bundle of clothes. Blondie held a pair of boots. Again, neither was visibly armed.

"Those for me?" Tom asked.

A window appeared in the cell, and they passed clothes and boots through to him. He stripped and got dressed in silence. They weren't his clothes. They were too clean. Too neat. He felt like a stranger putting them on. The boots hadn't been properly broken in yet, and they pinched his feet, but they didn't smell like a sewer so he considered that a win. To his surprise, when he reached into the pocket of the pants, he found a fresh pack of cigarettes.

A whole wall of the cell slid down, and he walked out, feeling fresher and better rested than he had in a week. A door in the room slid open and he walked through, finding himself in a long dark corridor. It gradually sloped up as he walked, Buzzcut and Blondie following close behind and silent, before ending at a security check. They waved him through, but not before handing him a new filtration mask.

"Be careful out there, sir. Pollution's been pretty bad the past few days," the guard said.

Tom ran his hand over the stubble on his face. "Thanks for the head's up."

"No worries. I've seen plenty of people get dragged down there, but you're the first one I ever saw come back again. Figure you must be important, and it never hurts to be nice."

Tom laughed and the guard looked confused but waved him through anyway.

Tom emerged into daylight, pulled his filtration mask up over his mouth and nose. The phone in his head rang.

"Hey, sis."

"They told me you were getting out today. Look across the street."

Tom looked up. Standing next to a car was Shari and Sunny both. "I'm going to guess I'm in trouble, huh?"

"Oh you could say that."

Tom made his way across the street through the traffic, flipping off the one car that decided to honk at him. Shari wrapped her arms around him, nearly staggering him.

"You've lost weight," Shari said.

"Uh, a bit. I wasn't eating all that well for a bit and prison food never agrees with me."

"So did you take them up on their offer?" Sunny asked.

"You know about that?"

"I guessed. You told me right now."

"Yeah, they did. No I didn't take them up on it."

"Why not?" Shari asked.

Tom looked back at the Kanedex building, steel and glass clawing at the sky. "A golden chain is still a chain, right?"

"And Prometheus?" Sunny asked.

"Gone. Dead. Dismantled. Whatever you want to call it. I don't know if Kanedex was happy with their prototype run or not. Maybe, hopefully, it'll be a dead end." Tom got into the passenger side of the car while Shari slipped behind the driver side and Sunny took up the backseat.

"And if it isn't?" Sunny asked, her voice more insistent.

Tom dug into the pocket of his pants and found the cigarettes. As Shari pulled into traffic, he lit one off the flame from his finger. "I don't know," he finally replied. "I really don't know."

The End

Acknowledgements

To Mom and Dad, for always celebrating even the minor wins. To Michelle, for always keeping me humble.

To Sean and Islay, even if you don't fully understand why I do this.

To Kelly, for supporting me even if what I write is far and away from what you prefer.

Thanks to Brendan Daly, who has been reading my work since high school and never once suggested I quit.

Thanks also to Cameron Mount, C.J. Casey, Matt Spencer, and David Barclay for their continued support and for pushing me to keep writing.

Thanks as well to the writing crew on twitter and elsewhere - C.W. Blackwell, Scott Cumming, J. Travis Grundon, Rob Pierce, Anthony Neil Smith, Eve Harms, Serena Jayne, Suz Jay, J.D. Graves, Michael Reyes, Tom Adams, Mark Pelletier, Ran Scott, Anthony Perconti, Nick Kolakowski, Stephen J. Golds, Beau Johnson and Karen Heslop among many others. Writing can feel like a solitary gig a lot of the time. You make it seem less so.

Thanks finally to the gang at Fahrenheit for taking a chance on this work and on me.

About the author

Matthew X. Gomez can be found on twitter @mxgomez78 and at his website https://mxgomez.wordpress.com/

Other work of his has appeared in Pulp Modern, Kzine, Econoclash Review, and Grimdark. He was one of the two coeditors of the cult New Pulp magazine Broadswords and Blasters. He released his first collection of fiction "God in Black Iron and Other Stories" in 2020. He currently resides in Maryland with his wife, two children, and three cats. He has the extremely futuristic job of sitting at a computer and staring at spreadsheets most of the day.

More books from Fahrenheit Press

The Eternity Fund by Liz Monument

When Jess Green is recruited by The Unit for her unusual abilities, she hopes she's finally found safe haven.

Unfortunately life in Department Thirteen (Crime Solutions) is anything but. A sinister brotherhood are stealing human organs, and Jess and her uncooperative handler are put on the case.

Their quest takes them into the lair of a rich philanthropist and his beautiful, brilliant daughter who together run The Eternity Fund, anti-aging as it's never been known before.

Haunted by flashbacks and convinced that something within the organisation is dreadfully familiar, Jess finds herself recalling the shadows of her past, and wonders whether she will ever truly be free.

"A futuristic noir thriller that will keep you gripped to the very last page..."

Iteration by Liz Monument

Another gripping thriller from the best-selling author of The Eternity Fund.

Behind the perpetual cornfields and fast-maturing livestock of the world's most effective genetic engineering project, computerised efficiency has outstripped even the smartest human mind.

Famine, warfare, and the effects of natural disaster will soon be neutralised forever.

But when unexpected events suggest that the supercomputer in charge is conducting its own secret experiments, only one person guesses exactly where this could lead. And it's down to Dr Jennifer Munroe to convince her increasingly careless colleagues to listen to her fears.

Spanning two thousand years and told by three narrators, Iteration follows the consequences of computation on the world around us and on the future of the human race itself.

"Liz Monument is such an atmospherically accomplished writer. This is writing of a different class..."

King Of The Crows by Russell Day

"Oceans Eleven meets 28 Days Later..."

2028, eight years after a pandemic swept across Europe, the virus has been defeated and normal life has resumed.

Memories of The Lockdown have already become clouded by myths, rumour and conspiracy.

Books have been written, movies have been released and the names Robertson, Miller & Maccallan have slipped into legend.

Together they hauled The Crows, a ragged group of virus survivors, across the ruins of London. Kept them alive, kept them safe, kept them moving.

But not all myths are true and not all heroes are heroes.

Questions are starting to be asked about what really happened during those days when society crumbled and the capital city became a killing ground.

Finally the truth will be revealed.

"In terms of plot, structure and ambition, this is the most imaginative novel I've read in years..."

Know Me From Smoke by Matt Phillips

Stella Radney, longtime lounge singer, still has a bullet lodged in her hip from the night when a rain of gunfire killed her husband. That was twenty years ago and it's a surprise when the unsolved murder is reopened after the district attorney discovers new evidence.

Royal Atkins is a convicted killer who just got out of prison on a legal technicality. At first, he's thinking he'll play it straight. Doesn't take long before that plan turns to smoke—was it ever really an option?

When Stella and Royal meet one night, they're drawn to each other. But Royal has a secret. How long before Stella discovers that the man she's falling for isn't who he seems?

"A beautifully written, brutal & brilliant slice of hardboiled crime fiction. A Knockout."

Turbulence by Paul Gadsby

Accidentally shooting a civilian during a bungled heist was bad enough, but when they upset the local criminal kingpin as a result of their ineptitude, newbie bank-robbers Birty & Cole figured the best thing to do was split town, and fast.

Smart plan - at least it was till everything went south, again.

An armed robbery is an unusual event which affects the lives of everyone touched by it and in this tour de force Paul Gadsby traces the lines of influence and connection that run through the lives of the people unwittingly caught up in Birty & Cole's heist.

The story is woven through the lives and perspectives of many characters - everyone from the bank staff and customers who witnessed the raid, to the journalists covering the case.

This remarkable novel from Brit-Noir legend Paul Gadsby ignores the usual crime fiction tropes of 'robbers on the run' and instead becomes a vivid study into cause & effect that will keep you gripped until the very last ripple fades away.

"Gadsby has really come into his own with this book - the writing & the storytelling are simply superb."

Lightning Source UK Ltd.
Milton Keynes UK
UKHW011149200222
398912UK00004B/61/J